Other writings by Ronnie Govender:

Plays

Beyond Calvary
The First Stone
His Brother's Kee
Swami
The Lahnee's Pleasure
Off-Side!
In-Side!
Back-Side!
Blossoms From the Bough
Who Or What is Deena Naicker?
At The Edge
Your Own Dog Won't Bite You
1949
The Great R31m Robbery
Too Muckin' Futch

Prose

At The Edge and Other Cato Manor Stories
Song of the Atman
In The Manure
Interplay

Book the first

Wherein lurks the subtlest of hints of an
impending drama and wheretofor the reader is
gently apprised of who was who in the
Mount Edgecombe zoo; whenceforth issued their
respective anxieties, idiosyncrasies, quirks, foibles …
presaging a scenario
wherein shit is about to happen.

Prologue

Even at the tail end of the Sixties, when the beatniks were riding into the sunset, Durban, like other cities in the Republiek van Suid-Afrika, just did not swing. The city was blissfully unaware of the sagacious counsel of the King of Swing, Duke Ellington, 'It don't mean a thing, if it ain't got that swing.' Not only that, or perhaps because of that, even when the British Empire had become a distant, albeit nostalgic, memory for the sons and daughters of Britannia scattered around the globe, Durban and its environs remained the Last Outpost of the British Empire.

North of the city, plonked amidst rolling hills of sugar cane, lay Mount Edgecombe. But for the occasional grunts of the workers digging and clearing the soil or cutting the cane and the cranking and farting of the old sugar mill, it was just another somnolent little village. A very special brand of LAW AND ORDER saw to it that the only manifestations of the Age of Aquarius in the village were long hair and bell-bottomed pants. Flower Power was contained in the neat little gardens of the tiny company homes of the workers, in the huge lush gardens of supervisors and city councillors and sundry officials, and in the council gardens that adorned either side of the main road.

The Aquarian Spirit was free to roam as much it wanted

to as long as it didn't cross the physical boundaries, which were at first customary and later meticulously delineated in pigmentocratic edict. Your pigment was the ultimate factor that decided the location of your habitat. In short, everyone knew their place in Mount Edgecombe, as they did everywhere else in the OLD SOUTH AFRICA, and thus there was this very special brand of LAW AND ORDER. Be patient, those readers in the NEW SOUTH AFRICA who are wondering what this Law and Order was all about. All will be explained.

In this neck of the woods, nostalgia for Empire lingered on in the minds and hearts of that sector of its melanin-challenged denizens who had wanted God to Save the Queen's dominion even after the Boers had changed the Union of South Africa into a Republic. Their forebears had long ago sailed from the overcrowded tenements of a plague-ridden little island, celebrated in literature, not without a touch of romance, as the Sceptred Isle. With bulldog tenacity they had voyaged across unknown seas in search of fabled lands of milk and honey, of climes bathed in the scents of exotic perfumes and spices, and dusky damsels with their dulcimers. This Barmy Army took with them their cannon and their bloodcurdling cry, 'Rule Britannia!'

This Empire-inspired ethos lingered on a century later right here in sunny South Africa, even after THE LONG WALK TO FREEDOM had reached its inevitable destination and democracy had replaced their once zealously secured pigmentocracy which, until then, had ensured the maintenance of this very special brand of Law and Order. A decade later, retreating into their gated villages, the melanin-deprived would watch in horror and trepidation as the institutions of their pigmentocracy came tumbling down one after another. To add ironic insult to injury, the mental coup that took place after the completion of The Long Walk, in the nerve-racking early Nineties, had taken root even within the portals of a distinctly Victorianesque City Hall.

Horror of horrors – even the revered name of the city of Durban was being changed to eThekweni, can you believe! Within the once hallowed precincts of the City Hall adorned with imposing statues and gilded portraits of devoted Empire builders from Benjamin d'Urban, after whom the city was named, to Queen Victoria, a deeply venerated colonial heritage was now being unceremoniously swept under its once sumptuous but now somewhat worn red carpets by the New Democratic Order in an unseemly haste to rid Durban of its singular distinction as the Last Outpost. And in its place, no doubt, another banana republic would emerge, my deah, you mark my words!

eThekweni indeed! An act of crass ingratitude, as the pallid denizens of the once pristine Berea would have put it. If you stood atop the Berea, especially in the vicinity of Howard College, later to be transformed, again unceremoniously, into the University of KwaZulu-Natal, above the flourishing flamboyants, rampant weeping wild fig, jacaranda and acacia, mango and avocado and splendidly verdant yet meticulously manicured rolling lawns which surrounded palatial homes, you might be forgiven if you thought you were anywhere else but in darkest Africa.

Over these long years, the torchbearers of civilisation, with cheap, bountiful indigenous and indentured labour at their behest, had developed such pieces of wilderness into eminently liveable habitats, reserved, of course, for those considered civilised. That was the operative ethos – civilisation, not barbarism.

Ah, how cruel the fates! In time, with uhuru, it came to pass that the raucous melanin-enriched sector of the citizenry sought, with unseemly haste, to reclaim the spirit of the Zulu Empire by changing Durban's name to eThekweni.

eThekweni indeed! eThekweni – perhaps the only city in the world whose name begins with a small letter. That late lamented citizen of Durban, one Mohandas Karamchand Gandhi, whose religion advocated the jettisoning of the ego in the pursuit of moksha or the liberation of the soul from worldly ties, would have felt much gratification at this self-effacement of the civic ego. Even the Mahatma's legendary suppression of his libido among a bed of naked maidens played second fiddle to this narcissistic abstinence, if you will pardon the phallic resonance of that well-worn phrase. However, had the Mahatma known that eThekweni, in Zulu, meant the balls of a bull, he might not have been quite so approving. On their first sight of Durban Bay, the Zulus felt that it resembled the giant testicles of a bull. Of course, although a whaling station came to be established within its confines, it didn't mean that it automatically became the playground of the Sperm Whale.

At the best of times, name changing is a hazardous business. There were those sceptics who maintained that efforts at name changing didn't quite succeed in wiping out the legacy of colonialism. Names such as Windermere and Manning remain. The sceptics were inclined to the view that this inconsistency, if not blundering, was not surprising given the fact that the joker who changed the name of Grey Street, the heart of the Indian quarter of the former Durban, to Doctor Dadoo Street, didn't know his marbles, let alone his doctors. This venerated doctor who dedicated his life to the Freedom Struggle lived in Johannesburg, where that name would have been more appropriate. It is mind boggling that the name changer was not aware that another venerated doctor, Dr Monty Naicker, who gave no less to the Struggle, had his surgery in Grey Street. The stereotype, of course, would have it that everything Muslim was Indian and everything Indian was Muslim.

One does not know how Mahatma Gandhi would have reacted to Point Road, the heart of eThekweni's red light district, being changed to Mahatma Gandhi Street. Some, however, averred that it was a stroke of genius, given that the good Mahatma was dedicated to the saving of lost souls.

In those halcyon days, before uhuru, if you believed all those indignant letters to the press that followed the name changes, the law was very, very clear about keeping people in their place. There was no question, not the slightest hesitation, no cringing heart-wringing, about the death penalty.

Dear Sir,
This country is fast becoming a banana republic all because of those bleeding hearts who support the abolition of the death penalty. These criminals have to be horsewhipped and hanged if we are to have any progress in this country.

Dear Sir,
In the old days, we could walk without looking over our shoulders in such civilised places as Durban's Berea, Johannesburg city centre and the mountain slopes of the Cape. Now crime has increased and no one is safe anywhere. Why? No death penalty, that's why! For God's sake stop blaming apartheid for all the ills of this country.

Ardent letter writers all, straight out of a Graham Greene novel, seated in decaying hotels on moth-eaten, threadbare settees and worn wicker chairs, in once spotless verandahs whose gleaming walls were now sprouting moss and sundry fungi. Pale souls lamenting, over gin and tonic, the golden age just gone by when crime was nonexistent in their part of the country. Sacred ground. No melanin-overloaded welcome here. Law and Order. Hence, these days, the gated villages from Umhlanga to Bishopscourt to Sandton, sprinkled with a few BEEs, (for those not acquainted with post-liberation double-speak, BEE means Black Economically Empowered, whose rallying mantra is 'I didn't join the ANC to be poor'), resonate with the cry 'Bring back the death penalty!'

In the halcyon pre-1994 days, in the sanitised portals of power in faraway Cape Town, were regularly hatched and diligently executed laws designed to maintain Law and Order. You could only have Law and Order if people knew their place. For people to stay in their places they had to know who they were, and so the South African lexicon found itself enriched by exciting demographic designations such as Bantu, Asian, Coloured, Other Coloured, Honorary White and White/European.

In time these terms underwent the inevitable transmutation that comes with colloquial conversion thanks to the demographically enriched social whirlpool, muddied by class stratification, into which a variety of races were so rudely hurled either by remote design or historical accident. Thus it came to pass that the indigenous inhabitants – the San and the Khoi – were either referred to as Bushmen or Hotnots, or more frequently, together with the Nguni speakers, as Pekkie Ous; those of Asian descent (excluding the Chinese and the honorary whites, the Japanese) as Char Ous; and the

Coloureds (those who issued from passionate liaisons between the Wit Ous and the Pekkie Ous) were referred to as Bruin Ous (come to think of it, which Ou on God's good earth isn't a Bruin Ou, given that passionate liaisons across ethnic and racial divides have been going on from time immemorial?). This practice even filtered down with lexiconic irony into the consciousness of the melanin-blessed, who happily referred to one another as Char Ous, Bruin Ous and Pekkie Ous. The melanin-starved stewards of Law and Order were generally referred to as Wit Ous. The more imaginative and adventurous called them Honkeys.

The hallowed mantra of the melanin-impaired was SEPARATE BUT EQUAL. The effects of this lofty social endeavour are fairly well documented but for our very parochial and immediate purposes it behoves us to note its effects on Mount Edgecombe's two hotels, the White House Hotel and the Saccharine Hotel. Pekkie Ous were barred from all the bars (an idiom that made the rule easier to remember). Unlike Pekkie Ous, Char Ous together with the Bruin Ous had their own bars but they were barred from the Honkeys' bars.

On Sundays, in deeply humanitarian consideration because it was the Lord's Day, the Pekkie Ous, who were the chingalans and bar boys, were allowed to have their itshwala and sing and dance in the sunshine just outside their khayas in the courtyard, faithfully replicating that familiar tableau of contented slave social life which frequents the yellowed pages of colonial history. And unfaithful to that tableau, without putting too fine a pun on it, in the dark of night some forbidden fruit was being savoured, but more of that later.

When our libidinous legend unfolds, back in the Mount Edgecombe of the Sixties, the Pekkie Ous, Char Ous and

Bruin Ous knew their place and when the menials know their place you could wager your last penny that things would run smoothly and thus there would be order, my deah, order!

Chapter One

Kamatchi leant over the fence and shouted, 'Arreh, Koonthi!' Not getting an immediate response from her neighbour she shouted even louder over the long rusted sagging fence overgrown with the sussussky vine that separated the Muthusamis from the Koonjebeharies. The sussussky belonged to the calabash family and could grow to the size of an ostrich egg. It was a reasonably good additive to meat dishes, especially mince or mutton curry. It could also replace calabash in kunjekeerai, that mouth-watering dish made from dhal, sour herbs and green chillies. It grew throughout the year but the fruit hung in abundance especially in the full flush of Mount Edgecombe summers.

'Arreh, Koonthi! Vah dee!' The Tamil colloquialism *Vah dee* translated into Koonthi's language, Hindi, became *Hauoo re*, which in English means 'Come Here, You Strumpet!'

An already sweaty hand tried ladyfully to wipe away the beads of perspiration which ran down Kamatchi's forehead. A red streak appeared across her face as her palm quite unconsciously disturbed the koongum, the red dot that Hindu women wear as a sign of their unquestioned status as marital retainers. What's a marital retainer? Someone who cooks good food, cleans the house, looks after the children, makes the bed and lies on it waiting for her maharajah, even if he is arsehole drunk. It's a duty she is expected to perform right up to the fifth, sixth, seventh, etc. child.

Dress codes, like the dhowni which Hindustani women draped across their heads and the purdah which covered up a Muslim woman's sexual assets, were strictly adhered to by marital retainers in our somnolent little village of Mount Edgecombe, emphatic evidence that even the retainers knew their place in those days.

She had just finished lighting the God Lamp, making the beds and sweeping the council house provided by the Hulett Sugar Company at 'a nominal rent', which in real terms amounted to a not unsizeable portion of the chickenfeed the sugar factory workers were paid. Their existence was mortgaged to the lahnees in the manner of the coalminer in the Sixties song who lamented, 'You load sixteen tons and whaddya get? / Another day older and deeper in debt. / St. Peter, don't ya call me / 'Cos I can't go, / I owe my soul to the company store.'

Kamatchi was taking a break from cleaning and dicing the vegetables and putting the dhal on the stove to boil. The stove, made of cast iron, bore the trademark 'Welcome Dover', another signal of British imperialism's civilising influence. It was Monday, the day of Lord Shiva, the day of abstinence, and when the kids came home from school and later when the man of the house, the maharajah Muthu, came home from work, there would be hot vegetable curries and steaming manja rice touched with a stick of cinnamon, not forgetting the dhal sprinkled with fresh, fresh dhanya plucked from their lush vegetable garden.

An equally sweaty Koonthi materialised through the back door out of the virgin smoke that issued from the just-lit coal stove in the kitchen. In her house, her husband Boywa would be treated to chicken and aloo. Her day of abstinence was Tuesday, the day of Vishnu.

– *Arreh! Why you shouting like a cut fowl?*
– *How cut fowl can shout, pagli? You never heard?*
– *What?*
– *Poolmathie, man!*
– *Poolmathie? What Poolmathie?*
– *Next door Poolmathie! Ayoo, what a thing, man!*
– *What thing?*
– *Arreh, so bad thing! Never heard?*

The bad thing, it emerged, was that their teenage neighbour Poolmathie was being secretly visited during the day when the rest of the family was away by a long-haired young man in a flashy car. While, as Koonthi observed, he was a small fuller who looked like the Bollywood matinee idol Amitabh Bachen, Kamatchi was not to be fooled. Indeed she was indignant. 'Small fuller? What you think he doing by that house every day? Playing marbles?'

– *Ya, maybe you right, maybe his marbles big enough to play with now!*
– *Isn't same fuller play football for Young Springboks?*
– *Not sure, but looks like same fuller!*
– *We must tell Muthu and Boywa.*
– *Huh! They won't do nothing!*
– *Why?*
– *That fuller can score goals, pagli, that's why!*
– *Telling me! Looks like he can score in the bed too!*

They were disturbed at that guffawing moment so deliciously pregnant with tongue-clicking outrage at the latest village scandal by a singeing sound which came from the region of the stove in Kamatchi's kitchen. She ran off shouting, 'Ayoo, the dhal! The dhal boiled over!' It must be

11

made clear at the outset that the dhal did not boil over all that much in Mount Edgecombe. Yes, there was some gossip but not always at the risk of the dhal boiling over – that was sacrilege; the food had to be prepared just right before the men of the house entered their domain.

Yep, melanin-soused wives in common with their patriarchs knew their place in those halcyon days when this salacious saga unfolds.

Chapter Two

Things certainly ran smoothly for Mr So-So, the manager of the White House Hotel, or so it seemed to him before that letter arrived (there are none so blind as those who will not, no, cannot, see). Mr So-So's name might have been more appropriate to his Englishness had it included the conjunction 'and'. The barmen and waiters at the hotel called him THE LAHNEE but if they, the errant ones especially, had their way they would have called him Mr So-and-So, or even Mr Son-of-a-So-and-So. Not because he was a Wit Ou. Stands to reason that whether you were a Wit Ou, Char Ou, Bruin Ou, or Pekkie Ou you could still be a So-and-So – that decision was largely yours.

In fairness to him, and to get the picture as much into focus as possible, Mr So-So was not anything like your average Wit Ou. Sure, he voted for Helen Suzman's Progressive Party, as a handful did in those far-off days, and secretly thanked God for the Nationalists, the party that was responsible for that resounding Caucasian ululation SEPARATE BUT EQUAL. Unlike most of those goose-steppers, however, Mr So-So was, in fact, a lahnee who took an occasional interest in his menials until the intrusion of a Tennysonian episode into his otherwise well-ordered life, which we shall later relate in all its delicious detail. This shocking, unexpected experience would change him into something worse than a goose-stepper.

If you had encountered him after this cathartic metamorphosis in his personality on receiving that mind-numbing letter and if you hadn't known him before then, you might be forgiven if you believed that he was born that way. He wasn't. Those who knew him as a youth will vouch that he was indeed a very pleasant young man. He would even joke with the melanin-overloaded menials who had worked for his family, especially his nanny, Matilda.

In fact, it wouldn't be an exaggeration to say that there was a time when he actually thought that Matilda was his mother. She would often strap him on her back when she went about her chores, effecting a bonding that would remain until his adult years. Even now he loves the smell of carbolic soap because it was the soap that Matilda regularly used in her daily bath, not being able to afford the more expensive perfumed brands like Lux toilet soap. In contrast, he never remembered the smell of Lux, which his mother used, or of Evening in Paris, the cologne which his mother sprayed herself with before her frequent social outings. The So-So's had quite a task, in his late teens, getting him to use Lux toilet soap instead of Lifebuoy carbolic soap for his daily baths.

They say the initial change in him came about the moment he became the manager of the White House Hotel. While he was training to be a manager it was stressed that in order to be a good manager he had to keep the Char Ous and Pekkie Ous who worked under him in their place. His career came first and so he took this instruction to heart. Thus a hitherto jovial, but somewhat rude and crude, young man changed into a real lahnee. Still, he wasn't that bad until that Camelot moment in his life, which, of course, we will reveal at the appropriate juncture. For now we want to stress that this is one of the crucial elements in this torrid tale and we promise to handle it with utmost storytelling delicacy when that moment arrives.

Richard So-So was an Englishman, born and brainwashed. He not only wore a tweed coat and scarf and sported a handlebar moustache, he rounded his vowels and pointed his consonants with gusto, especially when, after the initial change had come about, he said things like 'You blithering idiot!', which was quite often. Indeed, in time the staff had graded themselves accordingly – Blithering Idiot No 1, Blithering Idiot No 2, and so on.

Inevitably, the Pekkie Ous, as the African menials were called, were placed towards the end of the roll call of the Blithering Idiots. And the Bruin Ous, who were the Coloureds?, you may ask. Na, the Bruin Ous didn't do this kind of graf – they were mechanics, welders and bricklayers – the Wit Ous made sure that their generally unplanned-for Offspring were placed just above the other darkies through another of their smart-arse edicts, the Job Reservation Act. The Act decreed that Char Ous and Pekkie Ous couldn't become accountants, engineers or even welders. It also ensured that the Bruin Ous couldn't rise above the status of artisans. No expense or effort was spared in the course of effecting such imaginative and meticulous social engineering.

The White House Hotel seemed to have been snatched from the English countryside and plonked on the highest of Mount Edgecombe's rolling hills of sugar cane. Its only concession to the harassed victims of the heat and humidity was a wide shady verandah which welcomed its regulars who sought to slake their aching thirsts. Supervising the Char

Ous and the occasional Pekkie Ou on the sugar plantations and in the sugar mill was thirsty work.

The Char Ous were like automatons. They didn't need supervisors. You just switched them on and they never stopped working. Some held that it was a cultural thing. They believed that it had a lot to do with tradition. It was a hallowed tradition – in those days, if the menials were caught doing stupid things like wiping their brow or taking a minute's rest from the backbreaking labour in the hot sun, they caught the lash of the whip, which, for better results, was dipped in brine. The whip wielders no doubt built up huge thirsts as they went about their dedicated responsibilities.

After such exertions the Wit Ous had to have an extra gin and tonic, old chap. Hard work, this business of turning the sugar into Green Gold. The Hulett Sugar Company had transplanted another striking edifice from Olde England, the White House Hotel, on to this piece of mamba-infested, sweaty subtropica in order to cater for these sundry souls who had given up their jobs such as Coventry Garden barrow boys to seek their fortunes in far-flung outreaches of the Empire but had ended up in places like Mount Edgecombe as overseers of sugar fields and sugar mills.

The White House Hotel was built in the Tudor style. It stood proudly in verdant parklike splendour and every evening, especially on Fridays when the menials were paid, its bars would ring with Bacchanalian cheer.

Especially in the Char Ous and Bruin Ous' bar, although in this part of the world there were not many Bruin Ous, some of whom felt they were superior to the Char Ous and the Pekkie Ous because they had far less melanin and had surnames like Dunne, Hulley, Ogle, Fynn and King. It must be stressed that not all who issued from such illustrious bloodlines were so deluded. It was inevitable that some who were fortunate to have inherited sundry unhaemoglobined corpuscles felt that they were a cut above those who were not thus endowed. In time to come, the latter would be referred to as Other Coloureds. Their fate would be decided by the ingenious but simple test of having a pencil stuck into their hair. It must be stressed that the test did not include pubic hair. If the pencil didn't fall out, your identity card duly bore the legend Other Coloured. Social engineering demanded extraordinary imagination.

Friday evening at the Mount Edgecombe Hotel! Lekker, eksê, lekker! Especially for the king of the revellers, one Chaka Ronnie. Chaka ran a bucket shop. With him you could bet on anything from horses to soccer matches to who was going to get laid next by the village Casanova or its Amitabh Bachen double, whichever image of raving manhood was your preference. Chaka never sat down. He sauntered, drink in hand from table to table.

– *Howzit bru, have a dop! What you having?*

– *Double cane, pint of stout.*

– *Me too!*

And with that Chaka Ronnie would yell at Blithering Idiot No 1, Sunny the Barman: 'Sunny! Hey Sunny I'm chuning with you, what you acting like you deaf and all?'

Chaka was Blithering Idiot No 1's best customer and they had an excellent rapport, taking the often below-the-belt ribbing in good spirit.

– *Hey Chaka, how many hands you think I got? You think I'm God, got eight hands what?*

– *My mistake eksê! Sorry I never bring the camphor and the coconut.*

– *Good thing you didn't, I would have broken the coconut*

17

on your head and lit the camphor on your tongue, you moegoe!

All that would issue forth in one breath as he poured out the patrons' various poisons with remarkable speed and dexterity, not spilling a single drop. Only the Blithering Idiot No 1 could call Chaka a moegoe and get away with it. Anyone else who dared even whisper such a slur could well find himself nursing a purple eye or a bleeding nose or, worse still, being thrown out by the chingalan, which means 'bouncer' in Zulu.

Chaka was always loaded with cash. It gave him a huge kick to take out his wad of notes in full view of every one and peel of the notes with a flourish especially when he was ordering drinks. His cash-flush received a sizeable flip when he met one Corduroy Bobby. Corduroy got his name from his love of corduroy pants. He always had them on whether it was icy cold or blazing hot, which it was for most of the time in this part pf the world.

Corduroy was a 'tube-lightie' or a lowly hit-man for the Crimson League. Everyone in the Casbah knew that you couldn't fool around with him. He was reputed to have single-handedly taken on four guys from the rival gang, the Ducheens, beating up the gang's head honcho so badly that for the rest of his life the unfortunate man couldn't tell the difference between his posterior and his elbow. Needless to say he was duly replaced by one who could. The Ducheens swore that they would get even. That was one helluva mission but as the egg-head observed, when an irresisitible force meets an immovable object, it's bound to result in a serious mass confusion between posteriors and elbows.

When you mentioned the Crimson League in the Durban's Casbah at the time, people took notice. The Crimson League rose from being a vigilante group in Grey Street to a Mafia-style extortionist gang run by some of Durban's most dangerous crime bosses, Daddy Naidoo, Pine Mohammed and Jeff Moodley. The difference between the gangs was that while the Ducheens had plenty of brawn, the Crimson Leaguers were much smarter, outwitting the Ducheeners everytime.

Chaka bumped into Corduroy one memorable Deepavali, the Hindu Festival of Lights. It was meant to be a time of moral regeneration but for many like Corduroy and Chaka it was a time for extra boozing, feasting and letting off big-bang fireworks. A fortuitous set of circumstances had brought these once complete strangers together. On the morning of Deepavali, Chaka rose early, had his customary oil-bath. It was a time for both inward and outward cleansing. He then set off for Durban to visit his 'connections' for the occasion, taking with him the obligatory box of sweetmeats. He did it in style, hiring a rickshaw for the long trip. The rickshaw puller was adorned with colourful head-gear and a permanent grin showing a set of pearly white teeth. Before the start of the journey, Chaka peeled off a note with a flourish and indicated in broken Zulu that there was more where that came from. He had choreographed the journey and the rickshaw puller was dead on cue. All along the way Chaka lit his big-bang Chinese crackers with his cigarette and hurled them into the air. As they exploded the rickshaw puller did a smart jig and a whoop. It was quite a sight.

Eventually they hit town, literally. His cousins thrilled to see him and a sumptuous meal awaited him. Before that, however, after Chaka had presented his delighted Auntie with the traditional box of sweetmeats, he and his cousins decided to have a celebratory drink at the Himalaya

Hotel in Durban's Grey Street.

Corduroy Bobby was seated at the far end of the long bar regaling his acolytes with his latest tough guy exploits. Chaka didn't like bullies. He asked the barman, 'Who's that ou? John Wayne?' The barman grunted, 'Be careful, you don't want to mess with that ou. When he finish with you, your own ma won't know you.' Chaka was tempted to take up the challenge but this wasn't his 'territory' and his cousin Babloo strongly advised against taking on Corduroy. Chaka was always ready for a scrap but he wasn't on home turf. If this was the White House Hotel, Chaka would have thrown down the gauntlet. The upshot was he heeded the wise words of the barman and his cousin Babloo.

Several drinks later, Bobby got himself arse-hole drunk. Chaka winked at the barman, 'Looks like that ou won't recognise his ma if she happened to walk in here now, would he?' The barman grinned. At that moment a group of guys from the feared Ducheens Gang walked in. The Ducheens were from down-town Warwick Ave and as we indicated earlier, they had cause to hate the Crimson League, and Corduroy in particular, with a passion. And right there before them sat the Crimson Leaguer who whipped their 'chommies'. What's more he was in no position to recognise his own dear mother had she visited him at that moment.

A tough bruiser pounced. He grabbed the practically comatose Corduroy by the shirt and was about to let fly with a punch which would have enabled Corduroy Bobby to become the first man to set foot on the moon.

Now there was one thing Chaka couldn't stand and that was when someone hit a man when he was down, except that in this case Corduroy was not just down, he was motherless. Chaka grabbed the Ducheener's fist before it could complete its lunar mission, and brought the beer bottle he was drinking from crashing down on the Ducheener's head.

All hell broke loose. The chingalans or bouncers were hastily summoned and peace was eventually restored. There were some broken ribs, cracked skulls, some blue eyes and fractured fists but Corduroy never forgot that Chaka had saved him from becoming the first man on the moon. They became firm friends.

It was Bobby who got him to be a runner for the Bag Boys. Bobby, like Chaka, had long ago learnt that if they joined the long queues of job seekers they'd be wasting their time, so they joined the growing legion of hustlers, spivs and gamblers instead. Their line of work took them to every race meeting at the Clairwood, Greyville and Scottsville Race Clubs at which the Bag Boys reigned supreme. Punters spoke their name with awe.

Not everybody could become a runner for the Bag Boys. The Bag Boys were headed by Sam Pillay a shy, softly spoken punter who always wore a suit and tie. Sam had resigned from the teaching profession when he realized that he could make far more money playing the horses. His lieutenant was none other Corduroy Bobby who worshipped the ground on which Sam trod. That was because Sam pulled him out of what Corduroy himself said was 'big shit.'

Corduroy had punted on the horses in a big way. He had an account with a bookie, called Honest Joe Buchinsky. Corduroy soon owed Honest Joe 'big time.' For a time Corduroy stayed away from the course, but you couldn't hide from Honest Joe. Late one evening, Joe paid him a visit in two black limousines loaded with hoods who all wore black fedoras, striped ties and sunglasses. Corduroy had enough good sense to know that he couldn't take on six guys who looked like lock forwards for the Springboks, all with broken noses and pockets bulging with what looked like Lugers. Honest Joe spoke softly, 'Listen my friend and listen carefully. You got till Friday. You don't bring me my money, you say good-bye to your family.' Honest Joe flicked the ash from his cigar, patted Corduroy on his cheeks, got into his limo and left in a cloud of dust.

It was big news on the racing circuit. Corduroy went to Sam. 'Bro, I know you make a lot of money. Somebody could hurt you bad to get at your money. You do me favour and I'll look after you. Speak to Honest Joe and tell him to back off. I know he'll listen to you. I'll pay him but I need more time.'

Sam was a gentleman. But he was also very wise in the ways of the world, especially the world in which guys like Corduroy and Honest Joe were the main players. He was also wise enough to grab an opportunity when it arose. The truth was, carrying as much cash as he did he was an easy target. Sooner or later some thug would pounce. He needed a body-guard. He not only spoke to Honest Joe, he paid off Corduroy's debt, which for him was 'small smacks.' Thus Corduroy was initiated into the inner circle of the Bag Boys.

They were called Bag Boys because they carried leather bags brimming with cash. Sam had worked out a strategy to outwit the syndicates and cartels that actually ran the sport, never mind its claims of strict control and accountability. They had established a network of grooms, work-riders, jockeys and trainers. Invariably they knew when a horse was 'given a shot'. To all intents and purposes, doping a horse was forbidden, but the syndicates had the doping stewards in their back-pockets. They were smart enough not to overdo it and the doping was a tightly kept secret. Not for the Bag Boys. They had their informers.

They also got to know when a jockey was planning to throw a short-priced favourite, when a horse which had not shown any form, was ready for its first win at long odds. They were well up on all the tricks of the trade. They kept such privileged info close to their chest. If it got out the odds would be snapped by the punters and the trainers and jockeys would ensure that the horse didn't win.

The Bag Boys would wait for the last second after the syndicate which had set up the race had struck. The Bag Boys would then hit every one of the bookies simultaneously. The bookies were obliged to honour the bets – and Deepavali! the Bag Boys had struck again.

Chaka took full advantage after Corduroy had introduced him to Sam. He faithfully carried a bag for Sam, but also placed his own bet. That way he not only got a nice commission but collected his own winnings. But, as they say in the gambling business, easy come easy go and Chaka was never able to hold on to his takings.

Especially when he was ordering drinks for all and sundry at the White House Hotel. The Blithering Idiots would really have a hard time of it keeping up with the orders, especially Blithering Idiot No 1, the barman Sunny, who had to serve Both Sides.

Both Sides? Hang on, it's never a good thing when the scribe gets ahead of his story.

Chapter Three

Never before in his life did Mothie have cause to visit the police. Almost everyone in Mount Edgecombe was a law-abiding citizen. Not only because it was the right thing to do, but also because going to the police station was almost as intimidating as going to the Non-White toilet at the White House Hotel. Although the stench from overflowing buckets could indeed render the unsuspecting comatose, it was still much less intimidating than the Non-White section of the Mount Edgecombe Police Station. If prizes were to be awarded for architectural intimidation, South African institutions of Law and Order would easily walk away with the top bet.

Thus it would be readily understood that like most of the other menials Mothie knew his place and obeyed the law to the letter. Some would say right down to the last full stop.

However, there's the rub, or rather the nub: a sudden, bewildering chain of events had left him with no other choice but to enter the Non-White section of the forbidding Mount Edgecombe Police Station.

Behind the counter in the tiny room were squeezed, first, a gynormous Sergeant Labuschagne, who looked like a battered Springbok lock forward complete with broken nose and cauliflower ears. It would have been totally inappropriate to pronounce his name the mellifluous

French way, LABOOSHAIN. Indeed, the Afrikaans version, LABOOSKAKNEE, appeared more appropriate to his Neanderthal appearance, and of course more appropriate for those unfortunate souls who came within his line of fire. Then just behind his right shoulder was an overweight Constable Ahmed Moosa, who looked like a bad guy in a Bollywood movie, or more like a samoosa – flab-ridden, ambling, with laboured exhalations that could be mistaken for Bollywoodish sighs (and you would be forgiven if you did, considering that this was the only effective artifice in the impoverished armoury of these limited thespians); and an equally flab-ridden Constable Musi Tshangaan, whose sagging pot belly looked more like belonging to an mpimpi (which is not very polite for 'informer') rather than to a soldier in an impi. It was a sight to scare the excrement out of law-abiding citizens like Mothie.

Samoosa shambled towards the counter. Samoosa took his time. He had already sized up Overalls. This ou don't look like a bad ou. This ou looks like he knows his place. In between measured breaths he wheezed without looking at Mothie, 'What's the Trouble, Uncle?' Char Ous have rescued such words as 'uncle' from the graveyard of bourgeois conformity, thus energising the English language. When a Char Ou says Uncle to you, he beknights you. Char Ous have yanked this word from its barren English moorings, given it a new dimension, given it the old masala treatment. When a Char Ou says Uncle to you, he is going beyond ties of blood. He adopts you in the manner of the shark you can encounter any day of the week in Grey Street: 'Uncle, I'm chuning you, genuine, genuine Rolex. You can sommer waai to China, Taiwan, Gujerat or even Nigeria, you'll never get a Rolex at this price! Sathiema, Uncle!'

What indeed was Uncle's problem? What was it that titillated the folds of the Samoosa's abundant paunch, and those, as well, of Musi and Labuskaknee into spasms of laughter? What was it that had forced Uncle to enter the precincts of the forbidding Mount Edgecombe Police Station?

Be patient, eksê. In South Africa everything takes time.

Chapter Four

*On either side the river lie
Long fields of barley and rye,
That clothe the wold ...*

The *wold*. For Mount Edgecombe's Lady of Shalott, this word from the celebrated poem was so romantic that it was positively erogenous, evoking, as it slipped through her lips, an almost orgiastic shiver – a shiver that ran down her spine beneath her long hair, now thinning ever so slightly, every time she recalled Tennyson's timeless ode to her idol.

Mount Edgecombe's Lady sighed as she combed her hair, carefully dyed to hide the greying strands peeping through ever so shyly and every so often. She sighed again as she looked down from her tower, the top floor of the Whitehouse Hotel. Ah, the romance of olde English, the romance of such names as the Lady of Shalott, a name given her during a teenage gadabout those many years ago at an exclusive private school for girls in Hillcrest. Bronwyn Mary-Anne Braithwaite was known as a junior lady of letters. She regularly penned poems of love and plays of romance.

Fate sometimes plays strange tricks. One of her schoolgirl plays which was staged at the end of year concert was quite prophetic. Written in a moment of great inspiration it was entitled 'And The Willows Wept'. It was about a young lady who lived in idyllic surroundings. A sparkling stream flowed through a garden profuse with roses of the most striking hues. On its immediate banks were willow trees whose tresses kissed the stream as it wound its way through the garden. It was on the banks of this softly murmuring rivulet that the beautiful Katherine first set eyes on the young man of her dreams. He swept her off her feet. She was so enamoured of the youth that she did not heed the advice of her parents not to be hasty. She allowed herself to be swept off her dainty feet by his fervent proposal. One of the most dramatic moments in the play was the scene in which she stoutly defended her suitor before her parents. Her father tried his diplomatic best. He doted on her and she loved him. Her mother also loved her, perhaps not in the unconditional way her father did.

But there comes a time in life when one has to take action, however unpalatable that action, and however much love is involved. Her mother was anything but diplomatic and her poor father had a hard time calming both of them. Her mother almost turned her out of the house while outside there was thunder and lightning and rain and gale force winds. She was prepared to hurl herself into the darkness, a frail but utterly courageous lover completely at the mercy of the raging elements, while in the background Beethoven's *Appassionata* played. In a stirring moment she actually opened the door. The wind almost blew down her father, who struggled to close it. Eventually she had her way. Despite her parents' misgivings, a grand wedding was planned. The wedding was to take place on the banks of her gurgling stream on a patch of rich but well-manicured turf edged by rosemary, sage, basil and thyme right in the midst of the swathe of roses. In the days leading up to the wedding she penned many florid poems of which the centrepiece was the willows, whose locks, flowing in the balmy breeze, softly sighed their approval of her eternal love. Her parents prayed for a miracle. Then just a day before the wedding the news broke that the young man was wanted by the police for massive fraud. It turned out that he was not of high breeding as he had pretended but a shameful low-bred mountebank. And so the willows wept. Although it was her play, she left it to the teacher to choose the cast. As things turned out she was chosen to play the part of the heroine. Of course, as far as she was concerned the choice was done on merit. The fact that her parents regularly made large donations to the school's coffers had absolutely nothing to do with it.

And here she was, Bronwyn Mary-Anne Braithewaite, author of 'And The Willows Wept', in a midden called Mount Edgecombe, married to Richard So-So, a ruffian beneath the gentlemanly veneer. Richard could never completely hide his low-class parentage, much as he tried to affect an upper-class upbringing several levels up from his father's humble origins as a Covent Garden barrow boy. This was evident, among other things, in the way he now strove almost to the point of hysteria to round his vowels and mask the Cockney accent he was pounded with as a child.

God, the man was indeed a mountebank. What, however, was more unbearable was not that his vulgar origins so easily surfaced in unguarded moments after the fourth double Scotch, but that his manhood for a long while in their barren marriage, especially after the Scotch, barely surfaced. Ah, where was her Sir Lancelot? – and at that moment, that wondrous Sunday, as she sighed and sighed and sighed and looked down from her tower, the second-floor bedroom of the White House Hotel, there he was –

29

> *He* strode *between* the sisal *sheaves,*
> *The sun came dazzling through the leaves*
> *And flamed upon the brazen* flesh
> > *Of bold Sir* Fanyana Ngcobo.
> *A* muscled *knight for ever kneeled*
> *To a lady in his shield,*
> *That sparked on the yellow field,*
> > *Beside remote* Mount Edgecombe.

All of eighteen, Fanyana Ngcobo, one day to become field colonel of the ANC's underground military wing Umkhonto we Sizwe, the Spear of the Nation. Right now, though, Fanayana's glorious spear sashayed ever so visibly beneath his white denim uniform, the standard wear of the menials, as he strode into the ken of our sighing Lady of Shalott. And magic was wrought that fateful, glorious Sunday morn under cover of avocado and mango trees. Our Lady stopped sighing. She caught her breath. There truly was her heroic knight in shining armour, wielding the handsome Spear of the Nation in such glorious abandon, for in truth Fanyana had never worn a jockstrap. Indeed, a strap big enough to house Fanyana's resplendent jock was not easily obtainable. Besides, he just could not afford one. Made sense though; freedom of movement costs nothing if you're not talking movement between Bantustans and the Republiek. Those were the countries indeed, in those fine old balkanised days.

That same evening Fanyana in his one-roomed khaya amidst the banana bushes (while Richard So-So was into his fifth Scotch in the exclusive gentlemen's lounge of the White House Hotel, regaling his regulars with tales of Merrie England) together with our Lady of Shalott was blissfully breaking with tradition.

She left the web, she left the loom,
She made three paces through the room,
She saw the water-lily bloom,

and as Fanyana plunged in his spear she cried out as she hit the high note of human existence. Verily the Big Bang couldn't have spewed unto the Milky Way such a galaxy of stars as she experienced in that explosion of ultimate passion. That glorious first night, as she felt the weight of unfulfilment lift from her slender shoulders, the Lady of Shalott uttered triumphantly into the bracing Mount Edgecombe summer night:

The curse of the Covent Garden barrow boy is no more
upon me!

In the stolen moments of erotic splendour that were to follow, our Lady of Shalott averred that she would no more look to Camelot. Was she completely free of the curse? Would she forever languish in orgiastic reverie hoisted aloft so joyfully by the Spear of the Nation? Would the son of a former barrow boy discover her dark secret? And if he did, would he pour arsenic into her gin and tonic? What would be the reaction of Mount Edgecombe's melanin-diminished denizens to this disgraceful liaison between a Pekkie Ou and one of their own kind? Would they don Klu Klux Klan spook outfits, burn crucifixes, and castrate the heathens for so defiling their pristine womanhood? Worse still, what would the law do when it discovered that this heinous crime was committed right under its very nose? More importantly, what had this Tennysonian episode to do with Mothie's complaint?

Patience, dear reader. We have said it already, things take time in the New South Africa. In the days of Law and Order in the Old South Africa speed was of the essence, to the extent that conscientious cops did midnight sorties hiding in the boots of cars and under the beds of those daring to taste forbidden fruit.

In the circumstances, would this dark, nay, gloriously technicoloured, romance come to a swift, disastrous climax? Patience, patience! All will be divulged in due course. Before that, however, we can reveal that the Lady of Shalott arranged for specially made jockstraps for her Sir Lancelot. That considerate act would help in some way to prevent his generous assets from being unduly noticed by other ladies in distress.

Chapter Five

Poor little Johnny
His mudda was dead
His fadda was a drunkard
Couldn't buy him bread
He sat by the window playing his banjo
Thinking'bout his mudda far, far away

As in the popular juvenile ditty of the day, sung exactly as spelt here, Johnny never forgot his Mudda, now firmly ensconced among the angels. He also never forgot his Fadda, the drunken so-and-so (not to be confused with the melanin-challenged one in this saucy narrative), now firmly ensconced in Hades. One day his Fadda tried to use his Mudda as a punchbag (most of his punches went flailing into thin air, though, such was the state of his inebriation). Johnny wanted to kick the excrement out of him but this was his Fadda, and Johnny was a Char Ou. Char Ous respect their Faddas even when they are arsehole drunk and beat the shit out of their Muddas. But although he was a Char Ou, on this final occasion something stirred in Johnny. He recalled the many, many times this had happened and after every beating his Mudda just carried on. Just carried on! One day Johnny said, 'Shit!' And he did kick the excrement out of his Fadda even as his Mudda tried vainly to stop him. All of which sort of conspired to put Johnny off marriage.

Johnny vowed that he would never get married. When Johnny took a vow he stuck to it even if it killed him, and it almost did. Once when the village bully taunted him, calling him a bainchod, meaning one who is incestuous, Johnny vowed that he would get even. And it very nearly finished him. The bully turned out to be a karate expert. He fractured two of Johnny's ribs until Johnny grabbed a Coke bottle, broke it on the counter and rammed it into his tormentor's face, shouting, 'Maatherchod!', which meant one who did Oedipal things to his Mudda. As the blood gushed from his face, the karate kid forgot his karate and yelled, 'Ärreh Maire!', which, in Hindi, was a heartrending cry for his Mudda. When the cops showed up Johnny knew that a self-defence plea would be useless. The karate expert was well connected. Johnny gave each of the cops a portable radio. They tore up the docket.

He also vowed he would get rich and not be a bum like his Fadda. He noticed that there were many Faddas like his Fadda. Not all of them were drunks, but nearly all of them were beat up by life, sort of zombie-like. When the lahnee said jump they jumped, never mind their big talk when the cane and stout were down.

– *You don't know me, eksê! Me I take no shit from nobody!*

– *For true?*

– *Never!*

The only ones the Faddas took no shit from were the Muddas, that's who!

Hell, he wasn't going to be like that! He wasn't going to take no shit from nobody, not even from the lahnees.

But first things first. He got himself a job in a factory in Pinetown as a packer and general odd-job man in a motor spares shop. He worked his arse off. One of his teachers once told him, 'You're a bright boy.' He never forgot that teacher. Mr Mickey Joseph. A serious man who seldom smiled. Yet Mr Joseph was somehow different from the others. Not because he spoke English better than any Englishman he'd heard, and not because of his peculiar first name. Was it Mickey or Michael? It could well have been the latter, but in all the official designations as far as he could remember he was called Mr Mickey Joseph.

He remembered a story he had heard about the time when Indians came to the country as indentured labourers. They couldn't speak English. The clerks at the immigration couldn't speak Tamil or Hindi, the more preponderant of the languages of the indentured labourers. Neither could they speak the lesser-spoken languages Urdu and Gujerati. The clerks were either stupid or too poorly educated to take on more challenging tasks in Her Majesty's overseas colonial service. It came to the turn of two Hindi ladies whose faces were covered in that traditional haute-couture piece of Hindu modesty, the mundhani in Tamil or the dhowni in Hindi, a part of the sari which was draped over the wearer's head, leaving just enough for nervous darting eyes to peep through.

The clerk said, 'What is your name?' Not used to speaking to strange men, the ladies kept silent. He repeated the question. Silence. Then impatience: 'What in blue blazes is your damn name?' The first lady whispered to her friend, 'Thum bole' (which in Hindi means 'You tell'). The second said a little emphatically, 'Nay, thum bole' (which means 'No, *you* tell'). The slightly bewildered, but not so slightly arrogant, clerk wrote, 'Surname: Thum Bole.'

'You're a bright boy.' Mr. Joseph seemed to have said it in an unguarded moment as a sort of sudden response to something or other the 10-year-old Johnny had done. He couldn't remember what it was but he remembered the compliment, the only one he ever got at school. He was always getting into trouble. He hated all the other teachers because they were so ready to pounce on him, so ready to judge him, so ready to mark him out as if he was something he knew he wasn't. It was almost claustrophobic. They were part of the things that closed in on you. Like the Law and Order of Suid-Afrika. And the persistent pedagogues didn't just close in on you with voices dipped in the brine of hysteria, they whopped you good and solid. It seemed as if they were born with a cane in their hands. He didn't so much mind the whopping although it hurt. What hurt even more was the way they closed in on you. Like Destiny. Like the Dark Clouds of Nowhere. At times like this he could understand why some of his fellow inmates skafed. They filled their lungs with clouds of Durban poison, which designation was an international plaudit for the potency of Durban's much celebrated variety of the cannabis weed which grew in such abundance throughout the province of Natal. They thus desperately sought escape into a world of their own by inhaling the smoke of this foul-smelling weed.

Yeah, good old Mickey Joseph! May his Catholic God bless his soul.

Johnny did so well at the spares shop, they promoted him to salesman. He got to know every teeny-weeny, itsy-bitsy spare part. When a customer asked for a carburettor jet valve for a 1952 Chev he didn't have to refer to a manual. He went straight to the shelf. That took some doing when you're talking hundreds, no, thousands, of spares. You're not just

36

talking Chevrolets. You're talking all the different models in Fords, Toyotas, Datsuns, Citroëns, Volvos, Peugeots and Morris Thousands. You're even talking Mercedes Benz, Daimlers, Jaguars. He was enjoying his job, until 'this wit ou joined us.' It's a bit of a story, this experience with the wit ou and what made Johnny quit pursuing legitimate employment; we promise to go into the colourful details at the appropriate juncture. Suffice it to say that the upshot was that Johnny duly hit the rackets. As Blithering Idiot No 1 (Sunny the Barman, in case you've forgotten – and I don't blame you, with so many characters peopling this audacious anecdote) was to tell the Stranger, 'Don't worry about this fuller, bru. He's a lahnee. You want to buy a radio, tape recorder, those dirty books they keep underneath? See Johnny.'

See Johnny, indeed! Johnny had become his own man, his own way. To the regulars at the White House Hotel and other bars in and around the district, Johnny, star centre forward for Young Springboks, was also a fahfee runner and, although he was an emissary of the Chinaman who owned the fahfee franchise, he was very much his own boss. Of course, the hotel and pub owners turned a blind eye because it was good for business. Johnny made a neat cut out of being a runner but this was a front for his other more daring escapades, which some would deem illicit. In the main he was a fence for stolen goods such as watches, portable radios, car radios, 'anything, daddyo, anything! Even the dirty books they keep underneath! Where they show all the private parts and all? You name it, Johnny's got it.' The fahfee job also provided a sort of captive clientele for these pre-owned goods.

Johnny was a streetwise kid who dressed the way he talked – 'snazzy, man, snazzy' – long hair down to his shoulders, bell-bottom pants, immaculately shining Florsheim shoes without a fleck of dust on them, luminous nylon shirts. He drove a bright red Ford Mustang. Everyone wondered how he could own one when even the stinking-rich local bus owner Mustafa Mohideen couldn't. Simple. Johnny was in touch. He kept his ears and eyes wide open, some would say even in his sleep. One day at the races a sad looking pook-eyed Wit Ou who had lost everything was peddling his genuine Rolex watch. Johnny was quick to grab the chance. He put up the cash – a hundred bucks for something that cost big, big money.

Better than the bargain, the Wit Ou took a shine to Johnny. Over a couple of dops, which Johnny in his big-hearted but strategic way paid for, the Wit Ou (who assured the worried barman that he was actually a Bruin Ou in order to gain entrance into the Non-White pub) told Johnny a tale of woe. Turned out the Wit Ou's vrou was two-timing him with his best friend. One day he flattened his best friend's proboscis. His wife hit the ceiling. She cradled her lover's rearranged face in her arms and shouted blue murder. She demanded a divorce there and then. To spite her the Wit Ou decided to sell up everything, including his Ford Mustang, for a song, rather than 'let that cow get her paws on my cash'. Johnny pounced. When Johnny drove down the streets of Mount Edgecombe he turned his tape player on full blast, playing a genuine masala mix from Elvis Presley to Mahommed Rafi. His personal favourites were 'Jailhouse Rock' and 'Khabi Khabi'.

Needless to say, the car attracted everybody's attention, including the young ladies as they peeped from behind the elaborate lace curtains which adorned their windows – that's all most of them could do – the sexes were kept strictly apart in those days. As Mothie was to later recount, 'Our days can't see one girl with one eyes. Six o'clock all the doors must be closed.' This, to a large extent, even applied in Johnny's time, about four decades on from Mothie's days as a laaitie.

But whatever the age, the ways of the flesh have always brought people into conflict with convention. So it was with one generously endowed young lassie in Mount Edgecombe. In fairness to her she was not, unlike other young lassies in the district, drawn by Johnny's flashy Mustang. She had just stepped out of the sandy path that led from her house on her way to the main road to buy the bread and milk from Mohammed's Cash Store, which had a sign prominently posted below its masthead reading 'Please don't ask for Credit as a Refusal may Offend', which was slightly different from the sign in the bar of the Saccharine Hotel which read, 'Yea, though I walk through the valley of the shadow of death, I fear no evil for I am the meanest son of a bitch in the valley. So if you know what's good for you, don't ask for credit.' The young lady had just stepped onto the main road when Johnny drove slowly past. She didn't appear to take any notice. But Johnny certainly took notice of her. As he was to describe her later to Blithering idiot No 1 and the Stranger, 'She's lekker, eksê. Crazy pair of legs, long black hair and crazy tits.'

Who was this lekker chick? What role was she to play in this steamy saga? Was she the femme fatale who would eventually snare our confirmed bachelor Johnny? What did all this have to do with Mothie's complaint? Was Johnny that fuller who drove a nice moto-car, who looked like Amitabh Bachen and whose marbles were big enough to play with? Was she the young lady who was being gossiped about over the sussussky vine?

Patience, dear reader, patience. All shall be revealed.

Chapter Six

In the recounting of the lives of the dramatis personae of this lascivious legend, we are unable to reveal the name of one of its major characters, the Stranger. For reasons that will probably become clearer as this impenitent account unfolds, depending, to a large extent of course, on your intelligence quotient, the Stranger shall remain a Stranger. The primary consideration, however, is that, in keeping with the canons of melodrama, we are constrained from fully identifying the Stranger. We happily do so at this point as it certainly helps to give this piece of titillating theatre the edge that all good dramas are supposed to have, except to observe that in his masturbating years he had ever been given to pondering THE QUESTION THAT HAS BEEN ASKED EVER SINCE ADAM WAS INDUCED TO TAKE A BITE FROM THE APPLE –

WHAT THE DING-DONG IS LIFE ALL ABOUT?

Yeah, what the ding-dong! The only moments life 'swung' for him, it seemed, was like that celebrated existential moment when Jean-Paul Sartre heard a blues singer on the Left Bank. One can't, of course, guarantee that the great man hadn't had a skafe before his deep encounter with soul singing. Such an uplifting moment for the Stranger, it seemed to him, was the climactic moment of his jerking. All else was empty, mechanical, absurd. He had searched for answers in many, many books written by the world's greatest writers, gurus and philosophers. He was particularly moved by Shakespeare. Now if you read Shakespeare properly, the way the Stranger did, you would understand just how ding-donged Shakespearean prose really was. Indeed, a few decades after the Stranger's time, a distinguished Shakespearean scholar called Professor Pauline Kiernan came to the conclusion, in a quite remarkable book called *Filthy Shakespeare*, that Shakespeare was a very dinggy guy. Dinggy? Yes, like in the song which went 'My ding-a-ling / Your ding-a-ling / I want you to play with my ding-a-ling.' She provided adequate literary proof that when the great man used words like *Dance*, *spur* and *fast* he really meant the act of dingging.

So what has that got to do with the question: WHAT THE DING-DONG IS LIFE ALL ABOUT? Plenty! As Adam's snake crept up on her, Eve might have agreed that dingging was what life was all about. And no less a head-shrinking authority than Sigmund Freud would have agreed.

Yet, for those with thin skins like the Stranger, however ecstatic the high point of dingging was, when that brilliant moment had passed, the experience was transient and still *don't* answer the question. Unlike Durban's melanin-starved he believed that there was much wisdom in the words of Duke Ellington, the High Priest of Jazz who had said, as we mentioned previously, 'It don't mean a thing if it ain't got that swing.'

Not even the Bard, with all his dingging metaphor, could provide that swing for the Stranger. Dingging metaphor? Now to aver that the Bard was pornographic would be

41

considered by the purists as sacrilege. One cannot ignore the purists of this world, although the Stranger was inclined to the belief that they had messed up and continued to mess up the world. Thank heavens for people like Pauline Kiernan who help to put these purists in their place. Contrary to their predictable verbal histrionics at such literary heresies, as Pauline has pointed out, this was not to do this collossus of letters, and indeed of all literature, a great disservice. Kiernan concludes that there was no one more able to present the human condition on English stages as acutely as Shakespeare, precisely because England at the time was soaked in bawdiness. What better way, then, to pierce the general consciousness than through the metaphor of the times?

Nonetheless, what made the Stranger sit up in bed? Was it a sharp object in his bed? Was it Shakespeare's dingging metaphor? Was it a nightmare? Why did the Stranger react the way he did later on in this story? Most importantly, what role would the Stranger play in this audacious melodrama? By now you know our immediate response to these compelling questions – patience, patience, patience – all will be revealed in due course, depending on how fast a reader you are. However, if you are one of those smart alecks who skip to the last chapter to avoid buying the book, we'd like to say we know what the ding-dong you are all about, you tight-fisted creep.

Chapter Seven

The first toy that Blithering Idiot No 1 remembered receiving, on his fifth birthday, was a car carved out of wood by his father Kista, which was short for Kistensamy. Kistensamy himself was begotten of Chellakooty, who hailed from Hyderabad, India, a place etched in Kista's memory although he had never been there and although it incongruously still retained its Muslim colonialist name. When he was a child he had heard many times over about how his great-grandmother was one of the brave band of women who featured in the Telengana Women's Uprising against the marauding Muslim colonists, who diligently lopped off the heads of those who refused to convert to Islam or the heads of women who refused to sleep with them. Chellakooty was proud of the fact that his family was one of the families who refused to bow before the sword of Islam.

Thus Blithering Idiot No 1's real name was Sunny Chellakooty. He was also known in the district as Sunny Barman. People were often designated by the jobs they did – such as Baboo Builder, Naidoo Teacher, Rent Office Ganase, Moorkoo Auntie, Samoosa Samoodeen.

Sunny never forgot that toy car and for the rest of his life cars were to be a passion, even if he could barely afford a second-hand one.

His father, Kista, was a man of great ingenuity. Being desperately short of money was no big deal. He was very good with his hands. As Mothie was to tell Sunny later, 'Hell your father, Kista. What a good thunee player! Me and him used to play partners. Nobody could beat us in Mount Edgecombe.'

To digress a moment. Astonishingly, there are those who still don't know about the myriad gifts to Western Civilization as a result of Vasco da Gama's Discovery of India and Alexander the Great's previous Conquest of that land of spices and wealth beyond imagination. This ancient domain, whose civilisation will be even more adequately described by the Stranger when That Moment arrives, gave the world notation, language, chess, yoga, and (apart from bridge) that other card game, thunee. In Mount Edgecombe, if you couldn't play thunee you weren't a man. Quite often money was involved, but whether for cash or love, the game was played in deadly earnest and raging gusto, sometimes even ending in blows.

From Kista's vegetable garden came a steady supply of veggies and his fowl pen brought forth a regular supply of eggs and fresh chicken for the dinner table at least once a month. Kista's green fingers were to be marvelled at as much as other parts of his anatomy, which appeared to be equally gifted and which thereby enabled him to be just as adept at making babies. But he was a modest man, ascribing his achievements, especially when a new baby arrived, to divine generosity. He would say after a good few shots of cane, 'What to do? God gave.'

Whenever the opportunity arose, Blithering Idiot No 1 would recall Kista's several achievements. He would tell anyone who cared to listen, 'You know, the old man was good, man! He only had Standard One education but he became the foreman at the Sugar Mill. He was the chairman of the Silver Stars Football Club, a trustee of the Mount Edgecombe Temple, secretary of the Mount Edgecombe Thirukooth Dance Company and a member of the Mount Edgecombe School Building Committee. Top of that he had fifteen children.'

Being a Mount Edgecombe man born and bred, Blithering Idiot No 1 seldom mentioned the harassed, overburdened bearer of those fifteen children, Chinamma (a total misnomer if ever there was one, as it meant Small Mother). Chinamma was not only adept at childbearing. She could make a damn good russum – that delightful broth from which sprang the colonial colloquialism 'mulligatawny', another one of those distortions of the world's oldest living language, Tamil. 'Mulligatawny' was the Colonel Sahib version of *mulga thunee* meaning 'chilli water', again a total misnomer for that delectably spiced culinary marvel russum, which was anything but simply chilli water. Even to call it a soup, under which designation mulligatawny appears on Western-type menus, would be doing it a grave insult. Of course, your palate had to be capsicum-literate to savour this utterly delicious dish made from tamarind, fully husked garlic, ginger, dried chillies, sliced onion, whole pepper, seervum or cumin and kadu or black pepper seeds. Marinthe selvu, a combination of medicinal spices which was part of the diet to strengthen women after they had given birth, was added for a special russum when one had a cold or the flu. There was nothing better to soothe the fires of a babalaas or hangover than expertly made russum. Mind you, it took kai rasee, gifted hands, like Chinamma's to make a spanking good russum.

Patrons at the White House Hotel, including many melaninless ones and even Mr So-So ('Damn good mulligatawny soup old chap, whot!') who were fortunate enough to have been introduced to it, looked forward to Chinamma's russum every Friday evening, which they bought for just three pennies a glass. Chinamma's russum was celebrated up and down the North Coast and even down in Durban. Chinamma also made vade, moorkoo, manja-braised broad beans and kudle, which those of North Indian extraction referred to as chunna. Except for moorkoo, with all of them the tongue would suddenly be deliciously ambushed by the sting of dried or red chilli. Vade and kudle were made from chickpeas and moorkoo from pea flour. There was also fresh masala-fried fish and fishcakes loaded with green chillies. After a couple of shots of cane dashed with stout, there was no better bite than any one of these mouthwatering chilli-bites. Indeed, Chinamma's chilli-bites and russum were just as eagerly anticipated as the dops on Friday and Saturday nights by the menials of Mount Edgecombe.

Saturday night! As Mothie was to regale the Stranger eventually, 'Saturday night, jolling night! Arreh, what big, big prayers we'll have. Wedding! Big, big wedding we'll have. All Mount Edgecombe will be full up. People coming from Durban, Sydenham, all over. Full, full – Saturday night, all night Dancing! Arreh, all night Dancing. Your father Mandraji fuller, right? And me, I'm Roti fuller, right?'

To the uninitiated, or as Kista would have it, to the Muddas or the ignorant, Mandraji was a North Indian jibe for a Madrassi or a Tamilian from Madras, while a Roti fuller was a South Indian counter for a fellow from North India, where the staple diet was roti or unleavened bread.

Fate had conspired, or rather the British Empire had,

to bring together a Mandraji fuller and a Roti fuller from different parts of faraway India here in Mount Edgecombe to turn out the Green Gold. Together with an abundance of the yellow gold in the hands of the wizards of plunder such as Cecil John Rhodes, such assets engendered two societies, one the melanin-deprived, which could afford swimming pools, and the other the melanin-endowed, which could not afford drinking water. The special brand of Law and Order referred to earlier was to ensure that this division remained in place for many, many years even after the Long Walk had reached its destination.

As observed earlier in this canny chronicle, whether he or she was a Mandraji or a Roti, a Char Ou went about his graf like an automaton. But even automatons need a break. And when the sun went down in Mount Edgecombe of a Saturday, the menials, drivers, clerks, supervisors and some local small-time businessmen and hustlers would let off much pent-up steam. As Mothie was to reminisce, especially after a glass or two of wine at the Whitehouse Hotel: 'Saturday night! Your father, Mandraji fuller right, and me I'm Roti fuller right? Arreh, but dancing time, we'll dance Natchannia together.'

At which point a fascinated Blithering Idiot No 1 would chip in, 'What, my father, too?'

Mothie would be in full flight. 'Yeah, I teach your father to dance. Arreh, chee! Chee! Chee! Sunniya not like today's dancing. Everybody will go in one dark room – biting in the neck, biting in the mouth! Or they'll put one fast music – then everybody ...' and here he couldn't resist the chance to demonstrate the Twist. 'When this leg get tired, thava they'll put this leg. Dancing *that*? Dancing **that**?

'Arreh, our time, man, our time. Girls can't come out of the house – so strict they was. Arreh, six o'clock all the doors will be closed. Can't see one girl with one eyes. That time boys must dance girls' part. Saturday night! Saturday night! Fire all burning one side. Thabla, saranji, all getting hot by the fire. Everybody will ask, Mothie came way? Me! Kisten came way? Your father! Everybody looking for us to start the wedding joll.

'You know these big, big shots from Durban, Sunniya – arreh, all will come and sit in one place. Drinking whisky, brandy, everything, man. You know your father will say, 'Put one number for them, put one number for the big, big shots.' Arreh, I'll say, why you not starting the joll? But where that fuller want to start? Give him one two dops then that fuller on the tops. Your father! Me too I'll stand by the big, big shots.'

We'll suspend the rest of this part of Mothie's absorbing account till the appropriate moment, to enable us to continue with our résumé of the enterprising Chinamma. Her russum had hit a high spot with Mr So-So to the extent that she was allowed, with two of her schoolgoing children, to stand at the entrance of the Non-White pub and sell her delicacies, bringing a few more shillings to augment the ever-strained Chellakooty budget. We might add that whenever Mr So-So cast his condescending eye on Chinamma's sensual slimness hidden underneath that most sublime garment of sexual subtlety, the sari, he felt a slightness under his pants, a slightness he had given up on in his own bedroom. He looked around quickly to check whether anyone had noticed his lecherous look – it was heresy to be looking at the melanin-blessed like that!

Chinamma cooked up a storm for Sunny's memorable fifth birthday, as she did with the birthdays of every one of her brood, making chicken biryani with dhal and sambals followed by payasau and aplo. Payasau! – an ambrosiac sweet made of sago and diced almonds and coconut. But if you asked Sunny what he remembered most of his fifth birthday, it was not what the old lady prepared for the party but that magnificent present his father had carved for him, the wooden toy car. Sunny pulled it along in the passage and on the verandah, sometimes on the side of the road, on wheels made of spliced cotton reels carved and painted to look like actual tyres with actual wheel caps. He was the envy of his mates. Sunny was generous – he let them all have a turn. One good turn deserved another, and quite often his friends would, in turn, share their sweets with him.

Sunny had a way with figures and more often than not met the financial challenges of fatherhood because he was adept at making a plan. Indeed, some of the more enlightened of his patrons in the Non-European bar would wink at each other as they said behind his back, 'That ou is a shark, eksê – he sommer knows how to make a plan!' Under more propitious circumstances he might have ended up an accountant. Even if the Job Reservation Act prevented Char Ous and Pekkie Ous from becoming accountants, Sunny entertained thoughts of being just as good as a bookkeeper. He had no choice but to forego any such ambitions, at least for the time being. To inherit the tenure of the council house from his father, he had to be in the employ of the Hulett's Sugar Estate, serfdom in perpetuity.

However, his proficiency with figures came in handy when he had to replace his father Kista after the latter's retirement as barman at the Mount Edgecombe Hotel. As Johnny was later to observe in unflattering terms of the hundred rands Sunny was paid every month by the White House Hotel, 'Peanuts, my bru, but I guess it's okay for monkeys like you.'

Survival demanded both resourcefulness and some measure of guile. How he had never been found out was a bit of a miracle. Whenever the opportunity presented itself he short-totted his patrons, mainly in the White bar, and on occasion when a well-to-do stranger entered the Non-White bar. It must be said he never short-totted his regulars in the Non-White bar. Whereas an unimaginative barman would get sixteen or seventeen tots at most from a bottle, Sunny could stretch it to twenty. He would mentally add up every tot he poured from a bottle and by the time the last drop was drained he had already calculated his own takings above the hotel's.

His wizardry at juggling figures also came in handy at stocktaking time. He had Mr So-So completely outfoxed, to the extent that every so often he would slip into the stock his own bottle of spirits. He was careful not to overdo it lest he arouse suspicions. Indeed, although he never said so, Mr So-So was quite pleased with his work.

Furthermore, the management did not extend credit to its patrons but there were occasions when a patron in both the White and Non-White sections ran out of cash at the height of alcoholic euphoria. Depending on the patron's reliability, Sunny graciously entered the debt into his little black book. When at the end of the month Sunny presented the tab to the hapless patron you can be sure that a few extra shillings were added on.

That way he was able to have just enough to pay the deposit on a second-hand Morris Thousand, not to mention paying the school fees, buying shoes for his kids when others had to walk barefoot to school, and buying the occasional sari for his wife from the annual sale at Naidoo's Silk Emporium in Durban. He loved it when at village weddings his wife was invariably praised for her good dress sense.

In his precious spare time, Sunny pored through the second-hand car section of the smalls after the lahnee had finished reading the hotel's copies of the dailies. Not that he didn't read the new car adverts. He read them passionately, building wonderful dreams of sitting behind a brand new Mercedes Benz or Ford Mustang like Johnny. But he was a realist and, sighing, he would turn to the second-hand car section. He developed an ability to read between the lines. When the ad used words like *fantastic*, *immaculate* or *perfect* he would skip to the next ad saying to himself, 'Think I'm a moegoe!' One day he came across an ad which read, '1949 Morris Thousand. One owner. Engine needs some attention.' He knew by instinct that this was the car for him. The engine was no problem. Kista could take a car apart from bumper to bumper and put it back again. Sunny himself was no mean mechanic. What's more, the price was cheap, with its ageing melanin-unentitled owner eager to get it off his hands.

One afternoon when it was his time off, he and Kista took two buses to reach the imposing address in Morningside. The first bus, Mohideen's Toofaan Express, farted along all the way from Mount Edgecombe right up to Umgeni Road, where they boarded a municipal bus. They sat among the last three rows reserved for Non-Whites, as was only proper, viewing the empty rows ahead of them. For Kista this was as normal as the sun rising in the east. Sunny occasionally harboured a vague idea that either the sun or the bus was wrong but he soon forgot it. His childhood dream of driving his own car was about to become reality and the anticipation was so delicious he could almost taste it.

The house, both majestic and intimidating, made of red brick with white wooden window frames and resembling a museum more than a house, looked down grandly past the gambolling monkeys in Burman Bush, over a sparkling Indian Ocean with its frolicking dolphins. Sunny nervously pressed the bell. A stern old man with the same bearing as Mr So-So appeared in the doorway and answered, '*Yes?*' Sunny stuttered, 'W-w-w-e came f-f-or the car, s-s-sir!' The man cuffed his goatee in his wrinkled hand and said with a polished hauteur, 'Didn't you see the sign at the gate? All car enquiries at the back of the house.'

Once at the back of the house, which looked equally imposing, where the car was parked amidst gigantic ferns and delicious monsters, the old man softened. Its coat of paint had faded slightly but there wasn't the slightest hint of rust. What's more, the tyres were almost new. Sunny got in and turned the key. The engine sparked to life instantly and it fairly purred. The owner told Sunny, 'You're a lucky man, Sammy. Never had any trouble. Yes, there seems to be a slight overflow, nothing too serious, I imagine.' The melanin-deprived man sounded just like a melanin-deprived man would. What redeemed him for Sunny was that he was an honest one. He was certainly no second-hand-car salesman.

The overflow problem was easily sorted out and the car ran like a dream. The only drawback for Sunny was the colour, which Kista described as sharki – somewhere between shit and khaki. He took it to his pal Murugase, who had a backyard panel and spray-painting shop. He had it sprayed green with yellow stripes. The aerial was made a bright red. When he drove it around Mount Edgecombe he would hoot at the slightest excuse and when he drew someone's attention he would smile ever so humbly with a look that said, 'Aw, it's really no big deal!'

He never lost the opportunity to tell people about his pride and joy, which he named after his wife in small letters just below the headlights: Ponamma's Pride. Much later he was to tell the Stranger, 'Bru, I tell you, can't beat a Morris Thousand!'

– *Yes, pity they don't make them any more.*

– *Yeah. But we go everywhere. One Saturday afternoon when I was off, the wife wanted to go town bioscope there by Albert Cinema to see Sivaji Ganesan and Savithri in* Neela Malai ThiruDan – *what a film, bru!*

– *Really! What does that mean?*

'Thief of the Blue Mountain. Sivaji, what a great actor – the way he cried in the film – real tears, bru! Anyway we got into the Morris, my whole family' – which, as Sunny said, meant his four sons, two daughters, his wife and his unmarried sister. When a Boere cop suddenly stopped them, Sunny told his kids, 'Duck away in the back.' But the cop had stopped him for faulty tail lights, not for overloading. Sunny apologised profusely. The cop growled, 'Next time you must check these things, jou bliksem.' A grateful Sunny thanked him just as profusely, calling him Sir yet again.

– *Yeah! All right, you coolie – you better fix it up. Next time I'll fine you.'*

Mothie shouted from his end of the bar, 'Hey, if that's me I pay the fine! Nobody call me a coolie or a bliksem – not even a cop' and walked out so that Sunny had to turn to the Stranger instead: 'These people get very happy when you call them Sir. Bet you if I didn't say Sir he'd have fined me.'

Now we wouldn't go so far as to suggest that such contumely as 'bliksem' or 'coolie' spat out with gay abandon by the melanin-deficient was at the heart of the Stranger's Hamlet-like disillusion with life, although it cannot be denied that it came pretty close to making him muller than a Char Ou deprived of curry for two days or a Wit Ou who sees a Pekkie Ou sitting on a Slegs Vir Blankes park bench. Eish!

Thus far, from what we know of the Stranger, it would appear that our man was a pretty cool customer. Well before the flower power generation blossomed in far off climes, the Stranger had attempted his own ushering in of the Age of Aquarius. Following his moment of epiphany, that Damascian moment when he sat up in bed, he decided that maybe the guy in the loincloth had it right. Love. Pure and simple. Love. Turn the other cheek. Make a pair of sandals for your jailer.

In the event it would seem hardly likely that he would be given to action that was precipitate. Without pre-empting the climax of our story we must warn our avid page-turners that fate has a nasty habit of inducing contrariness. Are we hinting at a drastic turnaround in the behaviour of the Stranger? Enough. This orgiastic tale will only reach its climax with controlled titillation.

We make a solemn promise, though – we will not spare you the mesmerising minutiae of that precise moment when circumstances (or is it fate?) force the Stranger, one way or the other, into decisive, dramatic action. We cannot at this stage let you in on whether that action was contrary to his convictions. In the meanwhile you just gotta hold on, baby!

For now, however, we will relent a teeny-weeny bit just to reveal that what made him sit up in bed was a sudden sharp shaft of common sense. When, especially in his masturbating years, he hinted at wanting to join the Natal Indian Youth Congress, his pater, a schoolteacher, rebuked him. 'Life's worse for millions. Just be grateful there's someone paying your school fees. That's your priority. Get on with your life – and another thing, get rid of that Che Guevara poster, you don't want to end up like him; and for God's sake lose that Free Mandela poster too.'

Paternal nagging didn't end there – it extended into the realm of religion, which the Stranger found himself averse to at a very early age. He couldn't understand why one had to break a coconut or rub ash on one's forehead, among other oblations observed with such serious thoroughness by the adults in his family. He was told in the authoritarian tones which adults adopt in such circumstances, 'Do as you're told!' He was just as stubborn as his old man and he refused to, even when the belt came out. The old man sat him down. 'There are many things in life which cannot be explained like ... like two plus two equals four. With time you will understand the Hindu belief that God is within you. You are too young to read and understand Sankarcharya or Krishnamurthi. Until then just shut your mouth and do as you are told.'

That should have been that, as it was for millions if not billions of others throughout time. He didn't want to be like those hordes who went to war over God. God, it was a strange God that sanctioned murder in His name! The Stranger was not one of those millions or billions. He was the Stranger and one day he would seek out the writings of Sankarcharya and Krishnamurthi. A seed was planted in the process, a seed that was to germinate in that moment when he sat up in bed.

One evening, after another bout of earnest jerking, he lay on his bed with that washed-over feeling of lightness which oddly reminded him of the ad, 'For after-action satisfaction, smoke a Lexington.' Next to his bed on the floor lay the newspaper with a large picture of a golfer receiving his trophy in the rain and there was that feeling again. He had looked at the picture for a long while; it struck him that a mere caddie called Papwa had whipped a world champion called Player. He thought a long time about the name Player, the loser, who, unlike the winner, the self-taught Papwa, had just come out of a warm shower and into the very English lounge of the classically appointed Durban Club. A quote describing the melanin-attenuated, from Olive Schreiner, another of his favourite authors, flashed through the Stranger's mind: 'Fancy a whole nation of lower middle-class Philistines, without an aristocracy of blood or intellect or of muscular labourers to save them.' Philistine, not Player! Whenever he saw the name Player on the sports pages of the paper, he hissed, *'Philistine!'*

He was close to labelling an entire tribe of the melanin-skimped as Philistines, when one day he read about wonderful things being done about the care of indigenous trees, plants and animals. Believe it or not, among the things that were as close to his heart as his jerking were pretty ordinary objects like trees, plants and animals. He winced every time a tree was felled for no justifiable reason. He read with increasing admiration about two souls whose mission in life seemed to be to let nature go its own way. Their names were Makhubo and Player. Player! He was to later discover that this Ian Player was not anything like his Philistine brother Gary, who didn't care that the illiterate caddie Papwa, who beat the socks off him, received his trophy in the rain. In fact, the Philistine's stock response especially to nosy newspaper people overseas was, 'It's not as bad as you think. Yeah sure, the races are kept apart. I tell you they may be separate but we are doing everything to make sure everyone is equal.' And, believe it or not, for a long time there were many who took this angelic little maestro of the golf links at his word.

Back home there was at least one who didn't subscribe to this weird notion, his own brother Ian Player. That's when it hit the Stranger. There was no rule in the book that said there couldn't be a real Player, a real sportsman. That's what made him sit up in bed – the realisation that not every Wit Ou was a Philistine. And the realisation made him feel big – not in a jerky sense, you jerk! It made him feel big in the heart, in the mind, and common sense told him that that was where the real battle had to be fought. And that indeed was what Sankarcharya and Krishnamurthi were all about. And so, well into the night, when the urge to jerk came on again more powerfully than before, he fell back into his washed-over mood of lightness and he dreamt that he was wearing sandals and a loincloth, smiling sweetly at a bulldog in a suit wearing a bow-tie. The bulldog had turned up its nose at him and snarled, 'Out of here, you half-naked fakir!'

A half-naked fakir indeed! By all things sacred, he should have told the bulldog to go take a leak in Buckingham Palace. But a strange thing happened in his dream. He couldn't believe himself. Here he was actually smiling at the cigar-smoking, brandy-smelling bulldog instead of telling it to piss off or even jerk off. What a dream! When he got up he promised himself that he must stop his own jerking off. Somebody once told him that too much jerking off could make him go soft in the head. For a while, scared off by possible cerebral vitiation, there was a hiatus in his comfort sessions. More importantly he found himself smelling flowers and smiling sweetly at strangers, especially at Wit Ous. The question, however, was, had the dream sunk in, right in there where, as the shrinks believe, behavioural changes take place? That's the million-dollar question which we will endeavour to get to grips with at the Appropriate Moment.

Chapter Eight

Sunday morning. Kamatchi dared not rouse Muthu from his slumber. His gravelly snoring interspersed with snorting, whistling and farting, in no particular order, had long since roused the household. Everyone in the household respected Muthu's right to snore loudly on Sunday mornings. Not that he didn't snore on weekdays, he did, but the Sunday night snoring was something special. It was inevitable – it was the day after Saturday night. As a consequence of the dedicated imbibing of liberal doses of cane spirits dashed with milk stout, the decibel count of his nasal exertions hit the roof in a bewildering cacophony of sounds.

When he did get up, around ten with the hot sun almost high in the blue sky, there was a cup of hot russum waiting for him on the kitchen table. Kamatchi was almost as good as Chinamma at making russum. He got up with a start. Shit! He'd better get ready – his team the Young Springboks was to play Mount Edgecombe Rovers in the final of the Arunachalam Knockout Cup. Muthu was the team's official coach. He ran to the window, shouting, 'Boywa, you up?'

His neighbour and soul buddy Boywa Koonjebeharie was the team's manager. Boywa shouted right back: 'Long time I'm up, choothia! So long I'm calling for you. Kamatchi never tell you what?'

– *Sorry, bru. Hell the way I dopped last night!*

In Mount Edgecombe, the more booze you could consume, the more you were a man. Koonjebeharie yelled back: 'Yeah eksê, me too. Hey, eksê we better get going. Took some heavy bets last night.'

– *You got the umkoo?*

– *Sssh! You want he whole district to hear, you moegoe? Come here.*

Babalaas or not, Muthu was down next to the sussussky vine in a flash. Boywa whispered, 'Yeah, got it last night. Tshabalala reckons his muti is guaranteed. Tshabalala reckons he's the best muti man around. He reckon he's gonna come to the game just to make sure.'

– *It better work after what we paid, eksê. You made a plan?*

– *Yeah. Three o'clock this morning.*

– *Where you put it?*

– *There under the goal posts. Me and Tshabalala made one hole. Nobody can see it.*

– *Hey, we must get some muti to help next door peoples. My wife chuned me, there's one laaitie come when nobody there.*

– *Yeah, Koonthi also chuned me. She reckon the laaitie looks like Amitabh Bachen. Smart car too.*

– *Smart car? Not a red Mustang?*

– *You thinking what I'm thinking? Can't be!*

– *Maybe. Our laaitie's a shark, but what a centre forward, huh? He reckon to me, bhai, this game two goals, I promise you, two goals.*

– *Goals or no goals, I catch him next door I'll break his legs. Next time can happen to my daughter, hell!*

– *After the game, moegoe, after the game!*

The whole male population of Mount Edgecombe, all one thousand five hundred of them, grandfathers, fathers, sons and grandsons, turned up for the game in the sweltering midday sun. Some came from Verulam, Tongaat and even Durban. Blithering Idiot No 1 arranged to take the day off. Mr So-So was most gracious; after all, Blithering Idiot No 1 was owed many days off. In any event, his Indian patrons would all be at the grounds during the lunch hour midday session. Calvinist doctrine had it that liquor could not be served on Sundays, the day when the Creator rested. The alcohol industry complained that this would cut into their profits. This wasn't a desirable situation. The liquor industry made regular contributions to the erection of imposing churches and continued to make generous donations for their maintenance. The priests even acknowledged this magnanimity in their sermons. The law was duly amended to allow the sale of liquor provided a meal was served with it. They were confident that the Creator would be happy if patrons did not consume alcohol on an empty stomach on Sundays, although some like Chaka Ronnie believed that they couldn't eat on an empty liver. The lawmakers were also certain that the Creator would be more than pleased that such imposing houses of worship were built from the proceeds of responsible drinking, a term that, in the years to come, would turn out to be much in use by the Liquor Industry in the New South Africa.

It seemed that they hadn't heard the story that was very well known among real believers, whatever the ratio of their melanin endowment. It turned out that God had come down in human form (it is said that He did that every now and then). He came across a black kid crying outside one such imposing church in Bethlehem in the Free State.

– Why are you crying, my son?

– They won't let me into the church.

– Don't worry, my son, they haven't let me in either.

Sunny took his two sons and his father along. He made sure that he parked his car where everyone would be able to see it. Chinamma stood at the entrance to the ground with two daughters selling her vade and moorkoo, popcorn and peanuts. Mothie and his son, Premwa, sat on the embankment next to Sunny and his kids. Also, there were Constables Moosa and Tshangaan, resplendent in their South African Police uniforms. Kaknee was not there because melanin-minimised players were not allowed to kick the same ball in the company of the melanin-full. In any event, he preferred rugby. Soccer was for sissies. Although there was no need to, both cops walked around the ground warning people not to encroach on the boundary lines. They ignored Chaka Ronnie, who had set up his bucket shop under a mango tree in the middle of the embankment on one side of the ground and was offering generous odds of 9 to 10 on the favourites, the Young Springboks. Everybody thought that Chaka Ronnie was mad but most of them did not know that he covered himself by offering even money on a Mount Edgecombe victory and five to two on a draw. In the event of a Young Springbok victory he would still make a profit. In the unlikely event of a draw after extra time and obligatory penalty shoot-out, he would make a really handsome profit. On the quiet, Moosa himself had put his money on Young Springboks. Chaka Ronnie was a man of scruple – he respected confidentiality.

The ground was festooned with flags and balloons. Before the main game there were novelty athletic events such as an egg race, a three-legged race for fathers, and a sprint race for grandfathers. Mothie fell during the three-legged race, clutching his chest. Sunny held Mothie in his arms, shouting, 'Fetch some water, hurry!' He had heard somewhere that water had to be administered when someone was dying. Mothie was whispering something. Sunny leant closer and said, 'What you say, Mothie?' Mothie whispered, 'Forget the water, get me some wine.' Miraculously, there was a doctor in the crowd. He pulled out his stethoscope while everyone held their breath. It turned out that it was only heartburn. The doctor said, 'Take it easy on the wine next time.' You could even hear the collective sigh of relief way over at the White House Hotel.

Prizes were sponsored by Madhan's Mutton Market and Ahmed's Cash Stores. Singaram's Super Sound System was hired for the day. Unfortunately, one of the speakers blew just before kick-off and there was a rasping feedback. That did not deter the enthusiastic MC and the equally enthusiastic crowd. The Chairman of Mount Edgecombe Football Association, Mr Gurriah Venketarajalu, welcomed the throng. It was a long speech which was largely unintelligible except for the concluding words, 'and I welcome one and all of you from the bottom of my heart.' The crowd erupted into laughter because over the scratchy mike 'heart' sounded like 'arse'. Although they never heard a word he said, they greeted every pause with loud cheers. Chaka Ronnie led the chorus with shouts of 'Hear! Hear!' after every supposed phrase. Chaka just had to keep his marbles sweet with the man who could have had him barred from the grounds for gambling. Of course, on the quiet the Chairman had placed a bet on a draw. He was the only one who felt this way. He didn't tell anyone else that Chaka Ronnie whispered that there was every likelihood that it would be a draw. Chaka had winked a little too knowingly. The Chairman was never one to ignore a hint, especially from someone as knowledgeable as Chaka Ronnie. Needless to say, it was in Chaka Ronnie's best interest if the Chairman won a few bob.

Even the women watched the game, from the windows and verandahs of their white stuccoed cottages with their green doors and green window frames and gardens of roses, snapdragons, dahlias and pride-of-India in front or from the back the fragrant curry-leaf shrubs, bushes heavy with bananas and grafted litchi, and mango trees with round and long mangoes almost hanging to the ground. They had a ringside seat.

Kamatchi and Koonthi were more adventurous and were actually settled on the banks among the males, with the unusually full support of their husbands. They wore saris that matched the colours of the Young Springboks. Kamatchi blew a bob-whistle while Koonthi rattled a ratchet. Their raucous behaviour elicited a sarcastic comment from one of the older women in the cottages who thoroughly disapproved of such undignified behaviour from the mothers of the nation. Which nation was in their minds was not quite clear. The old auntie said, 'Ayoo, see how they doing. Such a disgrace! They acting like young, young boys, not even girls!' The women within earshot agreed volubly while secretly envying them their obvious enjoyment. A thin ghoulish-looking middle-aged woman piped up, 'No respect they got, acting like that in front of the mens and all.'

Koonjebeharie and Tshabalala stood near the anointed goal posts. Koonjebeharie kept rubbing his chin and pushing back imaginary strands of loose hair. Tshabalala was chanting under his breath and constantly looking heavenwards. They did not notice the manager of Mount Edgecombe Rovers sneaking into the corrugated iron lean-to which served as a dressing room, with a strange-looking brown paper parcel at the stroke of twelve. However, it did not escape the notice of Muthu, who spat three times in the direction of the lean-to and silently prayed that their umkoo was stronger. Just before kick-off there was huge drama when Abdul Malik the left back and Baboo Sarkhot the inside right for the Young Springboks refused to take the field because someone told them that pig fat had been rubbed into the ball. The matter was settled amicably when the ball was replaced.

Both teams had also done well in the Soobrayen's League Competition with Mount Edgecombe Rovers heading the log but the Young Springboks had a game in hand. Mount Edgecombe had strengthened their team by signing on the towering Fanyana Ngcobo, midfield general par excellence. Fanyana turned out to be a born footballer. He wasn't the kick and run, dribble, dribble and hope-for-the-best type of player. There was nothing aimless about his playing. Neither did he do things merely through instinct. Of course, when the going was tight he reacted intuitively, but more often than not his fine footballing brain came into play. He broke the forward moves of the opposition by reading a move well before it reached his own half of the ground. Another thing about him, he seldom if ever lost his cool. He took a robust tackle in his stride and refused to be provoked, but he gave as good as he got after a dirty challenge. This quality stood him in good stead when life was to entrust him with a responsibility far bigger than a football.

Not to be outdone, the Young Springboks fielded three of the Dunne brothers and goalkeeper 'Black Cat' Bambata (who also worked at the White House Hotel) and their star centre forward, Johnny, Mount Edgecombe's own George Best. Johnny could sell a dummy to the best of them. Master of the dribble, he could slice his way through the toughest defences. Topping all that was that he had power in both feet, able to shoot from almost any angle.

What a cup final it turned out to be! Unfortunately, as much as we'd love to, giving a ball-by-ball account of that memorable game is out of the question – we'd be accused of going off at too many tangents. We gotta keep this story as tight as possible, baby. That's not to say that we might not be tempted into reliving one or two of the many exciting moments of this memorable match at some opportune stage. The muses of storytelling often play strange tricks.

Did Chaka Ronnie make a small profit or a big one? Whose muti, whose umkoo, would prove the stronger? Who eventually won the Arunachalam Knockout Cup? Did the laaitie with the red Mustang score two goals?

But, for the purposes of our bawdy tale there were even more compelling questions: Was the Young Springbok centre forward as Kamatchi and Koonthi had suggested, the lascivious lad who had caused such excitement over the sussussky vine? What had all this to do with Mothie's complaint to the police? Read on! Read on!

Chapter Nine

The one area of his life where Black Cat Bambata didn't play it safe was on the soccer field. When he was between the sticks he was fearless, throwing himself full stretch at the onrushing boots of hellbent centre forwards. If you consider that in those days the boots were made of thick, hardened leather with soles lined with metal studs instead of today's hard rubber or plastic, the wearers of those weapons of mass destruction would be more lethally entitled to the Nike slogan, 'Just do it!' It was more than a few times that those studs left their indelible legacies on different parts of the Cat's taut, wiry body, but he was as game as they come and he wore his several scars with the pride of a true warrior of King Shaka's legendary impis.

Otherwise he was a smiling, obsequious vassal. When Mr So-So shouted, 'Hey wena! Figa lapa! Tata lo bottle and faga it lapa,' which was the full extent of his Fanagalo, the Cat jumped to attention. He had been working as a bar boy at the White House Hotel for ten years and was going along quite nicely. He had been able to save some money after sending a fair sum to his family back home in Amatikulu. He had been able to buy himself a smart suit of clothes on lay-by from Moosa's Outfitters in Grey Street, Durban. He was always suspicious of Char businessmen, but he liked the suit. Moosa himself had assured him, as he had assured all potential customers whether they were Pekkie Ous, Char Ous or even Wit Ous, 'Hundred per cent wool, genuine imported.' In truth it was made in China of synthetic fibres. To Moosa, business was business. When the Cat eventually paid it off in full, he looked at himself admiringly in the broken mirror in his khaya at the back of the White House Hotel. So too did the housemaids.

It was Muthu who first spotted his instinctive goalkeeping abilities. During a lunchtime drink at the White House Hotel, Muthu stepped out of the bar shielding his eyes and making for the dreaded loo at the back of the hotel. In the yard the bar boys were spending their lunch break kicking a ragged ball around. The ball landed at his feet. He had had just two beers and although he was well past his prime he still retained some reasonable skills. Once a crack centre forward, he instinctively dribbled past two defenders. He was in a great position to score. He let fly at what he thought was an open goal. To his amazement, almost out of nowhere flew this cat, catching the ball in mid-flight. Then and there, Muthu talked him into turning out for the Young Springboks and Bambata had never looked back.

Other clubs took note but they couldn't poach the Cat from the Young Springboks until Mount Edgecombe Rovers made him an offer he couldn't sneeze at. Until then he had played for the love of the sport and not money. There simply was none. He felt it right to talk to Muthu. Muthu was a man of the world.

– *Maalini?*

– *They say they pay me ten pound every game.*

– *You got twelve pounds starting next game. How's that?*

– *Muhle! Muhle!*

The Cat didn't exactly tell Mount Edgecombe Rovers where to shove their offer, Muthu did that for him – with the same relish he felt whenever the cane spirits washed down the tang that was torched on his tongue by a piece of red chilli in Chinamma's vade.

Until Fanyana entered his life, the Cat allowed nothing to upset the otherwise even tenor of his life – not even when his clan's headman approached him for a monthly contribution of one shilling a month towards Inkatha, the feared rightwing Zulu nationalist party. The moment the good-looking youngster joined the ranks of the bar boys he smelt trouble. The housemaids no longer paid him the same attention. At the soccer grounds they were now talking about Fanyana Ngcobo, the brilliant midfield general who played as if he was born with soccer boots on. Worse still, it was whispered that Fanyana refused to pay one shilling a month to Inkatha. The headman had glowered but that didn't stop the infernal, eternal smile dancing on his handsome face. Fanyana had even influenced three of the five housemaids, who stopped paying the levy, evincing dire threats from the headman. The reaction of the rebellious housemaids was the same as Fanyana – they kept smiling.

The Cat was certain that one day those smiles would be wiped from their faces and he even told them as much. He tried his best to convince the housemaids that it was stupid to buck the headman. Just one shilling, that's all. Nobody knew what they did with the money. They heard whispers that the headman wore the best suits, had five wives and drove around in smart cars. What they did know was that if you didn't pay you would unexpectedly be set upon by knobkerrie-wielding amalaitas. Ask the other bar boy, the hapless Petros. Not long after he had refused to pay, knobkerries suddenly rained down on his head as he was walking alone in the cane fields. Petros's facial features, let alone his head, had been permanently rearranged. They couldn't tell exactly who did it but in their hearts they knew. Why expose yourself to such a terrible fate?

But the Fanyana spell was cast. Big trouble, big trouble. The Cat had always minded his own business. Now his world was no longer private. An intruder had invaded it. A handsome daredevil who could also play football just as well as he did. In fact, he had to admit to himself that the adoration of the fans had shifted ever so noticeably in Fanyana's favour. It was not long before Fanyana also bought himself a suit from Moosa's Outfitters. When Moosa told him the suit was one hundred per cent wool, genuine imported, Fanayana smiled and moved on, making as if he was about to leave. He had learnt quite young that businessmen were businessmen whether they were Char Ous or Wit Ous, although the Wit Ous were a little more polished in the way they ripped you off. At the time there were no Pekkie Ous or Bruin Ous selling suits. As he reached the door, Moosa called him back. He reduced the price by a third. Fanyana bought the suit, which was exactly the same as the Cat's. That was it! All his life the Cat had been a good man, a nice man with his only blemish being occasional cheating on his wife. When he heard what Fanyana paid for the suit his hackles rose even more. He told Fanyana that the Char Ou had taken him for a ride and one day he would get even with these Char Ous. Fanyana smiled and said, 'Businessmen are businessmen!'

When he bumped into Fanyana these days, and that was often, given that they were doing the same job, it became increasingly difficult to keep up the friendly banter. Something had to give.

Then fate intervened. The housemaids were whispering that there was something going on in Fanyana's khaya when everyone else was supposed to be in bed. Something unnatural. One day one of the girls had heard some strange screams followed by long lingering sighs coming from Fanayana's khaya. Later she heard a rustling, crackling sound like someone treading on the dry banana leaves and mango twigs on the ground outside. She peeped through her window. The moonlight darting through impending storm clouds barely picked out a white figure hurrying out of the banana bushes that shrouded Fanayana's room. Ghost! Ghost! She quickly pulled the curtains across her window. But the image lingered. The ghost seemed to have long hair just like ... just like ... no, it can't be ... Fanyana wouldn't be that stupid!

But such images do not just fade away. They dwell; and even as she swept and washed the floors of the bedrooms and the toilets and changed the bedding, she could see the ghostly figure before her. The picture took on a life of its own. There are no limits to imagination. In her mind she saw the ghostly figure being held aloft by the Spear of the Nation and she could stand it no longer. She had to talk to somebody and, as providence, or whatever takes a hand in such matters, would have it, she spoke to the Cat.

She said the ghost only visited when the Baas, Mr So-So, was into his sixth double Scotch in the lounge with his closest friends, cracking up at the lewd jokes which poured forth as liberally as the Scotch did. This was very puzzling. What had the Baas's convivial, after-work indulgences with his friends have to do with the mysterious appearance of a ghost amongst the banana bushes in the backyard of the White House Hotel?

The maid insisted that this coincidence occurred with the regularity of clockwork. Some things in life were very strange. Take for instance that feared creature called the tikoloshe. The Cat had first heard about the tikoloshe, a small, horned, hairy creature with the teeth of a tiger, when he was barely five years old. He had heard vivid descriptions of this terror from his elders. Although he had never seen one, the image had been imprinted on his mind from his impressionable youth on. Life was indeed very, very strange. They said that some people had the power to summon the tikoloshe, especially to deal with people who made them mad. If you messed with such people the tikoloshe was sure to visit you in the dead of night. Even if you were as strong and as brave as a lion you were no match for a tikoloshe. Not even bullets could stop these beings from hell. So you did your best to stay on the right side of people who could summon tikoloshes to do their bidding. However, for a price they could send the tikoloshe on your behalf to deal with people who messed with you. Thus if you had the money and if someone got in your way, you could puff up your chest, roll your eyes and say, 'Pasop wena, I'll get the tikoloshe to tear your heart out and to eat it, uncooked, no maybe with a touch of salt and pepper! Apparently tikoloshes are very particular about their culinary tastes.'

Life indeed was very, very strange. There were many, many things in life that could not be explained, like why should a tikoloshe not eat a human heart without salt and pepper? However, the Cat was far too busy trying to survive than to bother spending too much time on such awesome questions. The important thing right now was that he needed a tikoloshe to get rid of Fanyana. So he paid the medicine man, Bulala Tshabalala, to let his tikoloshe loose on Fanyana.

It cost him the proverbial arm and leg but surely it would be worth it.

Late one evening, Fanyana had finished all his chores in the bar. He had cleaned up together with the Cat, emptying and washing all the glasses, wiping and dusting the counters. Emptying the glasses was not such a big deal. The barfly Koodikaran, whom we shall hear more of later, and one or two of his mates were on hand to guzzle the remnants of the precious liquid. Sunny had locked up and given the keys to Mr So-So, who was steady enough to receive the cash and the keys and totter his way up the stairs to his bedroom. The Cat scooted off without even a nod. This was odd behaviour. Yet it struck Fanyana that for the past few days the Cat wasn't his usual smiling, friendly self although he was still very much the grinning vassal in the presence of the lahnee and the Madam. Fanyana went to the communal bathroom and poured the refreshingly cold water over his splendid naked torso. He sang his favourite song, 'Asimbonanga', the theme song of the Free Mandela campaign, as he stepped out of the chipped and ageing metal bath and reached for the towel. At that moment he noticed a piercing pair of eyes above fanglike teeth peering at him through the window out of the pitch-black night.

Not even the original Sir Lancelot had such nerve. Cool as you please, Fanyana wrapped the towel around him and grabbed the doogoo, the knobkerrie he always kept around him at night when he was not on duty – there were lots of mambas around, green and black, and it was necessary to be armed. He rushed out through the bathroom door to the spot outside the window. He heard terrifying hissing screams pitched at a piercing tenor alternating with deep growls with such a low bass they would have done justice to the best of the Ladysmith Black Mambazos; but the creature was not be seen, camouflaged in the darkness that shrouded the banana bushes and the huge trees behind the White House Hotel.

Fanyana sprinted outside just in time to see a figure darting through the bushes. With the towel slipping from his waist, his Spear of the Nation felt the chill of the night air, but that didn't stop him. His eyes, now accustomed to the darkness, made out the profile of a furtive figure. Fanyana took aim and threw his knobkerrie with the strength and accuracy of an Olympic champion. He heard a thud followed by a howl of pain, followed by the sound of desperately fleeing feet. A sudden quiet descended on the scene. It was then that Fanyana noticed the others staring into the darkness, wide-eyed and speechless until one of the maids screamed, 'Tikoloshe! Tikoloshe!' To which Fanyana, hastily placing his paws over his Spear of the Nation, responded in the choicest Zulu, 'Tikoloshe, my eye! For my money that was a skebengu wearing a cheap mask from Bassa's Bargain Bazaar.'

The Cat was forced to admit that this was the stuff of heroism. Not even a tikoloshe could get the better of this man. How in heaven or even hell's name could he beat him?

In the midst of his despair he remembered what the maids had told him about the ghostly figure that entered Fanyana's room in the dead of night after the Baas had had his sixth double Scotch in the private lounge with his friends. He hung around the hotel corridors until he was convinced that the Baas was so occupied. He stealthily crept into the backyard and hid behind the water tank on the verge of the banana bushes. There were banks of cloud which hurried across the night sky every now and then, casting patches of darkness across the face of a full moon. Although it was a warm night and he wore a battered trench coat, he shivered slightly. Even stout warriors have their moments of hesitation. The moon had just emerged from a thick cloud when he caught sight of the apparition silhouetted against the banana leaves reflecting the pale moonlight. And what he saw with his own two eyes he just could not believe.

Chapter Ten

It was a sultry weekday afternoon. Except for the barfly, Koodikaran Kannabathy, muttering about the weather and trying vainly to interest Sunny in current district gossip in the hope that he could somehow pry a drink from the unyielding fates, the bar was quiet.

As we shall see later, Koodikaran, for all his bedraggled appearance, had a certain sophistry if not a touch of the pedantic about the way he could speak English. He preferred, however, to chune like a Char Ou because it afforded an immediate intimacy especially when he was out foraging for a drink, which was for the better part of his life. He was charmed by the accent, the rhythm and the syntax with which Indian aunties sought to extend hospitality or reassurance with such gems as 'Have tea and go' or 'I'm only saying for a word, man!' The tone and phraseology of the former was far from that used by those alienated souls affecting English accents when they said, 'Wouldn't you care for some tea before you leave?' which really meant 'You can piss off for all we care.' In contrast, the Indian version meant 'Please, you simply cannot leave our house without having some tea.' In similar vein, 'I'm only saying for a word' really meant, 'Please don't misunderstand me, my words were not meant to hurt anyone but just to make conversation.'

It was in such a syntactical context that Koodikaran ventured, 'Heat is very hot today eh, Sunny?' Sunny dismissed him as he would a vagrant thought and turned to scanning the smalls of the *Natal Mercury*. He didn't choose to read the editorial – unlike Koodikaran, who loved reading the denser parts of the paper whenever he could get his hands on one. Generally the highfalutin language put Sunny off. This is not to do him any disrespect. The lofty sentiments expressed in those august columns either offended or just plain bored him. Their meaning often meandered, couched as they were in language aspiring to notions of either the King's or the Queen's English. Despite this, however, his disinclination to read the editorial piece was due more to having to cope with the immediate rather than to any cerebral deficiency on his part.

Mr So-So, on the other hand, read the editorials assiduously. It was gratifying to him that someone was alive to such grave threats as 'Indian encroachment into white areas.' Give them an inch and they were all over you!

He had just finished reading the paper, retiring upstairs for his afternoon nap. Koodikaran loitered, turning his attention to Fanyana who was tidying up the bar, ready for use by Sunny. There was something about the way the youngster moved that caught his attention. Every step was in tune with a predefined rhythm which, in Koodikaran's language, was 'like way out of here, bru!' This was a guy who could handle a football if he really wanted to.

Koodikaran, who once, before his fall from grace, was a more than ordinary footballer, a midfield 'fetch and carry' man to be exact, ventured some advice to Fanyana, almost tripping over himself as he sought to demonstrate a through pass. 'Must find hole. No hole, make one! Our days, when

I make like that Muthu must move to the hole. Thava goal!'
(a 'hole' for Koodikaran was what today's football pundits
would call a gap). A good midfield player, Koodikaran went
on, has to read the game and just know in this bones how to
make a through pass. Of course, his team mates have to help
create the gaps and anticipate the through pass. In football
parlance, the man without the ball is more important than
the man with the ball.

Fanyana smiled indulgently. He was used to getting advice
from the patrons, most of whom were ardent supporters of
his team. As he also did on the midfield, he had mastered
the art of being unobtrusive. He never got in anyone's
way as he moved about the bars on his various tasks of
placing the empties in crates, taking them to the storeroom,
washing glasses, wiping them and arranging them on the
shelf, sweeping and wiping the chairs, tables and counters.
There was no end to the hundred and one things he had to
attend to all day all over the hotel. He took it in his stride,
with more than enough energy left to rise to the occasion
whenever he was visited in the dead of night by the Lady of
Shalott. Fanyana was fully aware that he was living on the
edge – one slip and he would be hurtling down into an abyss.
He promised himself after every visit by the Lady that this
would be the final one. Whenever the Baas, as Mr So-So liked
to be called, decided to sit down for some drinks with his
special patrons, which was about twice or thrice a week, he
knew that the good woman would be paying him a visit.

He felt a growing inclination to break off the liaison, more
especially because of the inherent dangers. It could also blow
his cover. Cover? Patience, patience!

Our Lady was most persuasive and indeed not without
some appeal. She made up for the inevitable ravages of age,

such as her now slightly sagging breasts, with practised
seduction. She made sure she undressed in his presence before
the dim candlelight was doused. The flimsy black underwear
and the heady scents she wore gave her a somewhat flattering
allure. Besides, every time she visited, a five-pound note, in
the currency of the Sixties and at the going rate then, slipped
from underneath her bra. When Fanyana drew her attention
to it, she waved it away.

In fairness to her this was not meant for vulgar procure-
ment. It was her way of encouraging his secret ambitions,
which she was both amazed and delighted to happen upon in
the most unlikely way. At the height of their lovemaking, he
one day reached under his sagging choir mattress for a thick
book which he placed under her posterior to enable her to
provide greater thrust. After the orgiastic tide had washed
over her, she reached under her posterior to remove the book
and was astonished to discover it was a tome entitled *Roman-
Dutch Law*, Vol I. On another occasion he used *Native Law
and Administration*. How did these pieces of academia make
their way into that humble khaya? At first he tried to dismiss
her enquiry with the response that he had picked them
up in a second-hand bookshop. This did not arise out of a
sense of modesty. It was something far more practical. The
knowledge that an ordinary bar boy was studying law could
pose all sorts of problems. He was doing a correspondence
course through the University of South Africa for a BProc
degree, which would enable him one day to emerge as a
sort of junior lawyer. Although the Bantu Education Act,
which was intended (in Dr Verwoerd's words) 'to make the
natives hewers of wood and drawers of water', had not yet
been promulgated, poverty and a paucity of schools had
engendered massive illiteracy. There was also the possibility

that if management got to know they would fire him. The educated melanin-suffused were a hazard in more ways than one.

She questioned him at length, not only astonished at his academic achievements but also his steely determination to rise above his circumstances. Studying by post was costly. It must have taken a huge chunk of his measly salary and she was tempted to pressurise her husband into raising the salaries of the bar boys. But she knew that this was a waste of time and there was the possibility, even remotely, of evoking suspicions. She also felt the stirring of the long-dormant playwright within her. Of course, the hero of her epic would be Fanyana in all his physical and cerebral splendour. Her play would end with the discovery of his secret studying and their secret love affair. They'd both be burnt at the stake. What a melodrama that would make! It would outdo Othello. The title for the play came to mind instantly – *Alas, Poor Fanyana!*.

As he went about his duties in the bars Fanyana loved taking it all in. He never drank himself, but alcohol did seem to produce such good cheer although it often eventually reduced people like Koodikaran either to bumbling idiots or outright nuisances. Generally, once a few drinks were down, fascinating tapestries of human action and interaction emerged. Everybody loved everybody, even the loud and uncouth. There was much ribald banter and raucous laughter. There was conviviality in both bars but it wasn't quite the same. In the melanin-starved bar, no matter how loud the laughter, it appeared to be a touch forced, a touch jaded. While he took everything in he generally kept his mouth shut especially as he watched Sunny go about his business of craftily augmenting his meagre salary by expert sleight of hand. If Sunny duped the unsuspecting and got away with it, it wasn't his business. He actually liked it when Sunny pulled his neat little rip-offs in the lahnees' bar. The mlungus could well afford it.

But heaven help Sunny if he got caught! He would not only lose his job and probably end up in jail, but his family would also lose their company house. He had a great deal of affection for Sunny and promised himself that one day he would take him aside and warn him against taking such risks. In life one just had to play safe.

If he only knew this cautious side of Fanyana, the Cat would consider such a sentiment from Fanyana as being a bit rich considering the chances he was taking with the Lady of Shalott. By now he had ascertained that the apparition he had seen enter Fanyana's one roomed khaya was none other the Baas's better half, or, as a full-blooded specimen of outrageous masculinity in thought and deed like himself would say, the Baas's soiled half. The Cat's world was very much a man's world.

The Cat planned his next move carefully. He couldn't just go up to the Baas and say, 'Baas, your wife is being dingged by Fanyana.' One never knew how a cuckolded husband would react. The chances were that the man could become extremely defensive and loth to admit, especially to a Pekkie Ou, that another Pekkie Ou was dingging his wife. The Cat just didn't want to risk losing his job. After thinking about it for some time he decided that the best way was to write a letter to the Baas. The problem was that he could not write. Whom could he go to? At that precise moment, by remarkable coincidence, Koodikaran Kannabathy bumped into the Cat as he walked with a crate of empties to the shed outside the bar. Koodikaran stopped him. 'Hold on there,

Cat. Don't mind if I sommer make your load lighter?' And with that he checked the empties for minuscule amounts of residual liquor.

Fate had indeed delivered a letter writer to the Cat. He told Koodikaran that he wanted to warn a friend about his cheating wife. All Koodikaran had to do was to write a letter warning this anonymous friend that his wife was being dingged by someone else. Koodikaran said it would not make sense if the culprit was not named. The original payment for writing the letter was a pint of beer but the Cat made it two pints if he promised not to reveal to anyone that the Cat was behind the letter. For two pints Koodikaran would do just about anything. And so with a flourish he put pen to paper. Before his fall from grace, Koodikaran had worked as a junior clerk in a legal firm. The letter read thus:

Dear Comrade,
It is with a deep sense of regret that I find myself compelled to bring to your urgent attention that your spouse is engaged in secret, illicit coitus with one Fanyana Ngcobo, an employee of the White House Hotel. Circumstances compel yours truly from divulging the identity of the originator of this sad missive, but rest assured that this regrettable intimation has been issued in your best interests.
Yours faithfully, Anonymous.

Koodikaran might have felt that he had chosen his words carefully, but not as far as the Cat was concerned. Koodikaran believed that the word Comrade seemed appropriate because it not only meant a close friend but it was much in vogue. The Cat agreed that it was much in vogue not for the reasons advanced by Koodikaran but because, given the need for socialist solidarity amongst the melanin-overloaded, the word had found its way into everyday usage. A true comrade would die for you, if not for the cause, but if you stood in his way he would choose to kill you for the cause. Although he sometimes felt like that (the killing part) about the lahnee, the Cat was not happy with the designation 'Comrade'. It was too great an honour to bestow on him. Besides, Inkatha's politics were anything but socialist and the lahnee was anything but a comrade. The Cat was careful not to divulge who the letter was being addressed to. It was duly changed to Sir, although Koodikaran protested that one did not address a friend as Sir. However, his protestations fell away at the prospect of two beers.

The next problem was how to deliver the letter. For obvious reasons it couldn't be delivered by hand. That would surely give the game away. Koodikaran was tempted to say, 'For another two beers, I'll do it myself' but although he did not know the man the letter was meant for, the risk was too great. Koodikaran's thoughts waded through alcohol-numbed grey matter. In a few moments, after deep concentration, the alcoholic amnesia lifted and he shouted, 'I got it!' The Cat grinned in relief until Koodikaran said, 'It'll cost you another pint.' 'Hau, this chap is greedy but what the hell.' Koodikaran revealed his scintillating idea after a long pause and slowly widening grin of triumph. He announced, 'We'll post the letter, that's what!'

For the Cat this was just as suicidal as handing over the letter personally. He felt trapped. It was a big decision. He needed to think about it. He told Sunny to give Koodikaran a pint of beer on his account as he went about packing away more empties. All his life he had played it safe, which was why he regularly paid his dues to the headman although it grated him to do so. He always smiled graciously in his dealings with the Baas and the Madam, even when they scolded and berated him in those early days when he was learning the job. After much deliberation he came to the conclusion that there was no other way. Whether one liked it or not, life was full of risks. He realised he just had to put his trust in Koodikaran. To hell with it, even if it cost him yet another beer, he just had to take the chance.

Koodikaran was now the repository of the most explosive secret in Mount Edgecombe. His sense of self-importance soared. There was a newfound bounce in his step. What is it about people who have been vouchsafed with a secret, especially a secret as damning as this one? They seem to revel in the burst of power that comes with it, as if they had been marked out by fate to possess knowledge that could lead to the downfall of another human being, especially one regarded as being so highly perched on life's ladder of survival.

Chapter Eleven

It was a Tuesday morning when the lahnee sat at his desk attending to the many accounts that were delivered by post. He ordered a pot of strong black coffee. Before he'd finished half of it, he suddenly realised that far better than the coffee to banish a babalaas was Chinamma's russum. He always kept a quart bottle full of the stuff in the hotel's fridge. It was just as tasty either piping hot or ice cold. As he drank the russum, the thought occurred to him that russum was a far better cure for a hangover than even the best remedies from the chemist. He toyed with the idea of marketing the remedy, mainly in bars and bottle stores, in cardboard containers (plastic containers had not yet made their appearance in abundance). He imagined setting up a thriving business with Chinamma responsible for making gallons and gallons of russum. He entertained pleasant thoughts of keeping her in his employ. Perhaps then he would be able to take the slightness he felt in his pants whenever he was in her presence to its logical conclusion. It didn't even occur to him that she might not be that way inclined. He knew of course, at the time, that when a Char Ou married it really was 'for better or worse, in sickness or in health, until death do us part' – and certainly a death sentence as far as he was concerned. But he was the Boss, and would Chinamma's resolve to stand by her marriage vows not fade away with the possibility of Sunny losing his job?

Such thoughts continued to occupy him as he sipped the russum and opened his letters. He was about to open the next one when he hesitated. His hesitation was not born of any intuitive sense. Rather, he paused because the envelope was slightly creased and soiled and also because his name was written on it by hand in the most stylish letters. Whoever wrote it must have been a master calligrapher. Obviously this was not an invoice or statement. It must surely be a personal letter. He hardly ever received personal letters. He approached the envelope tenderly and patiently with eager anticipation, if not with delicious curiosity.

Before he opened it, he poured himself a pint of draught beer. In his long experience as an earnest imbiber, he had discovered that just as good as russum was the hair of the dog. He reminded himself of his perennial New Year's Eve resolution, to cut down on his drinking. He was not getting any younger, he told himself. Despite what he told himself, when he got going with his mates the resolution flew out the window. Who could blame him when there was so much conviviality, so much good humour around?

Last night, for instance. All he had meant to do was have just three double Scotches, no more. Then one of his mates who had just come back from England came up with a whopper. A Springbok lock forward was at a loose end in London. The anti-pigmentocracy rent-a-crowd had disrupted their scheduled game against England and they used the day sightseeing. The lock forward visited the London Zoo and noticed a kid taunting a lion in its cage. The kid made the mistake of putting his hand through the bars. The lion grabbed the kid's hand and would have mauled him but for the brave lock forward. He pulled apart the iron bars of the cage and he socked the lion right on the nose with a punch that would have flattened Joe Louis. The lion dropped down dead. Next day's headline in the London *Daily Mirror* read, 'Racist Pig Slays Child's Pet'. How could he stop drinking after that? He laughed again as he placed the letter on his desk and picked up the mug of draught beer. This was something of an occasion. He took a sizeable swig, wiped his lips, wiped his hands, and opened the envelope with great care.

As he read the contents his face turned an ashen grey. Beads of sweat appeared on his forehead and on his pockmarked nose. He grabbed the beer mug and hurled it against the filing cabinet. The explosive crash shocked the staff but they dared not go into the office. When the Baas was really angry he did that sometimes. At such times it was best to steer clear of him. It must have been an hour and half a bottle of Scotch later that he emerged from the room. The unnerved staff stammered that they didn't know where Fanyana was. They knew the lahnee liked his drink but never had they seen him this drunk so early in the morning. He was very wobbly and sweating profusely. It seemed, however, that he was making an almighty effort to control himself, to the extent that his voice came out in something of a piping contralto, a sort of hyena-like screech instead of the usual stentorian command: 'Sunny, will you see me in my office, immediately.'

Sunny was in the office before you could say Black Cat Bambata or Fanyana Ngcobo. He was startled to see the half-empty bottle of Scotch on the desk but even more to see the 9 mm parabellum next to it.

– *Yes, sir.*

– *I don't see that Fanyana Whatsisname around. Why isn't he at work? Where in blue blazes is he?*

– Sir, today is his day off.

Fanyana must have been born under the luckiest star in the whole wide universe. Indeed, this was his day off.

– Isn't he on the premises? For God's sake, man, it's your duty to know exactly where the bar boys are at ANY given time, isn't that so?

– Yes, sir, I mean no, sir, I mean …

– Will you shut up, you blithering idiot!

The lahnee slumped back into his chair with such suddenness that Sunny felt that he was having a stroke or a heart attack. This must be pretty serious. He ventured feebly, 'Sir, he's back on duty tomorrow morning. I'll tell him to come and see you first thing.'

'Yes see that you do that. If not …' The lahnee reached for his gun.

'Yes sir, certainly sir.' Sunny fled.

When Sunny got back behind the counter, a more than curious Koodikaran, also roused from his alcoholic somnolence by the explosions from the lahnee's office, asked him what had happened. Sunny was not usually given to discussing work-related matters with the barfly, but he was so unnerved that he blurted out what had happened. Koodikaran was shocked into sobriety. 'He got a gun, true's God?'

'Sathiemma!' Being a religious man, it was not often that Sunny took the name of God in vain.

Koodikaran felt he had to do something. He'd become mixed up in this whole business just to get himself a couple of pints of beer, not to get involved in murder. He was involved whether he liked it or not. He made up his mind then and there to warn Fanyana. He was careful not to speak to the Cat. Instead he found out from the maids that Fanyana had gone to the Post Office to collect a parcel of books. He rushed to the tiny Mount Edgecombe Post Office and was just in time to see Fanyana step out with a package in his hands.

Koodikaran described what had happened in minute detail. He begged forgiveness for writing the letter and he pleaded with Fanyana not to put his foot on the premises of the White House Hotel. Fanyana was not used to running away from confrontation, but Koodikaran continued to beseech him. 'You can't argue with bullets.'

The drunk was right! He couldn't go back. And so our hapless hero vanished for good from the sleepy little village of Mount Edgecombe. Ironically, as later events were to prove, it turned out to be a good thing for the country as a whole that he had to bring his careers as a bourgeoning footballer and as a lawyer in the making to a rude halt.

Back at the White House Hotel, on first impulse Mr So-So wanted to blow out his wife's brains. He burst into her room, gun in hand. The Lady of Shalott was seated at her favourite spot, in front of her winged mirror on her dresser, carefully waxing her chin. She was not in the least disturbed by the sudden intrusion, having long got used to her husband's oddities, crudities and complexities, especially when the drinks were down, although it vaguely occurred to her that it was still early in the day. She hadn't turned to see him, so she didn't see the gun. Then a sudden torrent of angry expletives issued forth in the choicest Cockney, bursting through the carefully cultivated upper-class English accent. Richard So-So had retreated into his Coventry Garden barrow boy alter-ego. As they say, you can take a man out of Coventry Garden but you can't take Coventry Garden out of him. He thrust the letter into her hands. She calmly read its contents and just as calmly put the letter down on her dresser, all the while looking through him at the farther wall.

When the Lady of Shalott had to, she could turn into the prototype of the English Iron Lady, made famous or notorious, depending which side of the Constructive Engagement discourse you were on, in later years by Margaret Thatcher. She didn't say a word. Instead she thrust out her chin as if to say, 'Do your darnedest.' Long years of cohabitation with the son of a barrow boy had given her a keen insight into his character or lack of it. She felt he just didn't have the balls, literally as well. She finally taunted him: 'Go on, what are you waiting for?'

That was a gamble. A cuckolded husband is no less dangerous than a wounded lion. His hand itched on that trigger, even more so at her total absence of guilt or remorse. His expletives exhausted, he searched for the right thing to say, which is always a difficult thing when anger clogs up the cerebral circuits. 'So you don't – you don't deny it?'

'Why in God's name should I?' the Iron Lady said calmly.

The gall of the woman! Now she was bringing God into this. Besides, did not God separate the races Himself, giving each one a colour that was different, noses that were different, the colours of the eyes that were different? He wished her struck down by a bolt from heaven for her blasphemy. For one moment, one fateful moment, it occurred to him that he might have to do God's work for Him. His finger tightened a fraction on the trigger.

Fortunately for her, in that brief time which seemed to stretch unto eternity, common sense cleared up the clogging of his mind; the good Lady of Shalott was fortunate not to collect a bullet in her cranium or another delicate part of her anatomy. Richard was almost certain that he could get away with shooting Fanyana, but he would not get away with shooting his wife. Even in a near-apoplexy he felt he was obliged by pigmentocratic convention to behave in a way that would not let the side down.

And so reason prevailed. In the circumstances it would appear that only a few people knew or had suspicions about the affair, whereas her killing would see her adulterous adventure being splashed across the front pages of the newspapers. On top of the disgrace of having let the side down and the further disgrace of being exposed as one who couldn't satisfy his spouse, to the extent that she had to run to a Pekkie Ou, he would lose his job. Instead, by mutual agreement, she was shipped back to the land of her forefathers, the mighty Sceptred Isle, where some shrewd investments of her own ensured her independence. She did not in the least mind the separation after so many years of barren marriage. What she missed were the rolling hills of sugar cane being gently caressed by balmy breezes in the Mount Edgecombe sunshine, and most of all she sorely missed the Spear of the Nation.

Was this the end of this tragic episode? In the sense that the Lady of Shalott and her Sir Lance-a-Lot went their separate ways, perhaps. We say perhaps because wouldn't it make for a great novel if chance had them meeting somewhere on the Sceptred Isle? This was not beyond the bounds of possibility considering the mention earlier in this intriguing mystery that Fanyana was to become field colonel of Umkhonto we Sizwe in exile.

Be that as it may, for the purposes of this scurvy account we are left with a vastly different Mr So-So or, dare we say, a Mr So-So of a vastly different hue. Was this the final nail in the coffin that resulted in a far more acidic and emphatic manner in which he now rounded his vowels and pointed his consonants especially with words such as 'You Blithering Idiot'? Wait and see! Wait and see!

Book the second

How the drama of Mothie's complaint unfolded
one afternoon when the heat was very hot in the
Non-White bar of the Mount Edgecombe Hotel.
In other words –
The incendiary force of the eventuating shit
was such that it even hit such faraway objects
as the sussussky vine.

Chapter One

The company homes of Muthu and Boywa were an undulating hill away from the White House Hotel. Both Kamatchi and Koonthie, when they were not breaking their backs with housework, would every now then observe the people who were going in and out of the hotel. They didn't need binoculars, they had both good eyesight and rich imagination. More often than not there was much to provide ready material for gossip, like the time Koodikaran came staggering out and vomited all over himself and the roses that adorned the garden. The burly chingalan got him by the scruff of his neck, hosed him down, made him hose the vomit off the roses, and then threw him off the White House premises.

Kamatchi and Koonthie were so engaged when they spotted the Red Mustang drive up and park on the gravel in the section reserved for the melanin-favoured. Johnny got out, dribbled and shot for goal with an imaginary ball, then whipped out his comb and combed back his long hair, which the wind had ruffled through his open windows. He was not a selfish young man. He kept his windows open so that the whole district could hear his music as he slowly drove down the main road.

Kamatchi drew attention to the car. 'Isn't that the same fuller?'

— *Which fuller?*

— *Pagli, that fuller who can score in the football ground and in the bed.*

— *Looks like him, no?*

— *He goes to the bar every afternoon, but I never saw him drunk one day.*

— *Ya, one thing he not like Koodikaran.*

— *No, you putting the cart before the horse. Koodikaran not like HIM. When a man gets drunk like that he can't get up to mischief.*

— *For true, eh? When you that age, making love is more sexciting than drinking. I wish Boywa was like that.*

— *And I wish Muthu was like that too.*

Both of the women sighed with faint memories of the sexcitements of yesteryear. They expressed their curiosity about what actually went on in the hotel. Yet, no matter how fecund their imaginations were, they could never have expected the drama that was soon to take place within its walls.

Earlier we mentioned the Both Sides that Blithering Idiot No 1 had to serve at the Mount Edgecombe Hotel. In the days when there was Law and Order, this architectural conundrum was a necessity in all on-consumption outlets. The law had it that the drinking area for the melanin-undercut be separated from the area for the melanin-improved. The size of the clientele at the Mount Edgecombe Hotel was such that, while it was quite sufficient for a neat enough return, it did not make financial sense to have to employ two full-time barmen in two separate bars. In effect, this would have meant actually employing three barmen, one being a relief barman, given the long hours. So a dry-wall partition was erected separating one bar from the other. A door was strategically placed in the partition to enable the barman on duty to serve Both Sides during his shift. This would mean there would then be only the one relief barman, making good financial sense.

The Hulett Sugar Company, which owned the hotel, was not wanting in good monetary practice. After all, this underpinned the rampant success of the British Empire, and indeed of all other European colonisations. To this day, the enormous monumental buildings in all the major capitals of Europe with ceilings and statues that reached to the skies celebrating the founding fathers, mothers and armies of European colonialism bespeak a highly developed skill both in unrestrained militarism and bewildering diplomacy. Indeed, Jesus Christ might have been tempted to react with greater physicality than he did with the money-changers, had he realised that His name was not just evoked in vain, it was evoked most effectively for gain. As the late great Professor ZK Matthews put it to the descendants of the melanin-enfeebled colonists, 'When you people first came here, you had the Bible and we had the land. Now we have the Bible and you have the land.' That state of affairs would ironically remain as such even long, long after the Long Walk had reached its destination.

In sharp contrast, the Indian-cum-Coloured pub at the Mount Edgecombe Hotel was shabby and run-down, the furniture makeshift. Strangely, this did not stop it from somehow exuding the atmosphere of an English country pub.

The heat indeed was very hot that day when the Stranger entered the bar for the first time. He was about thirty-five years old and neatly dressed. He looked around, peering through a window that looked out over the sugar mill, the lifeblood of the town.

Johnny had chatted with Sunny around midday regarding his activities at the White House Hotel and then left. Sunny, neatly togged in his barman's outfit – white shirt, black tie and black pants – had just ushered Koodikaran out and gone to serve the melanin-restricted. On his return he saw the Stranger looking out of the window. He turned to wiping and arranging the glasses on the counter. The slight tinkle of the glasses drew the attention of the Stranger, who turned towards the counter and said, 'Oh, there you are barman. Nice little place you have here, reminds me of an English country pub, er, except for the enamel tables – somehow same kind of atmosphere.'

– *It's awright, bru. What can I get you?*

– *Double cane and coke.*

– *You waai'd overseas and all, huh?*

Yes, London, the Stranger said. A busy place! Not as busy as the bar when the workers finished work at the sugar mill, Sunny told him, especially over weekends. 'These fullers get paid Fridays. They buy their sweetmeats there by Goolgoolah's Sweetmeat House, they leave it by the house and then they come here to have their poison. I get so busy.'

– *Do they give you any trouble?*

– *No, no trouble nothing with these fullers, man. You know, bru, twelve and a half years I'm working here, not one day any trouble.*

– *Twelve and a half years, gee, you know something, in another twelve and a half years you might get yourself a gold watch.*

– *My lahnee will give it to me, man.*

– *Your ...?*

– *My boss, man.*

– *Oh, yes, yes.*

The barman warmed to the Stranger, and confided that he'd learnt his trade from his father who had worked at the same bar. Sunny had started as a wine steward. 'You know how much scolding I used to get from my father, bru? Old man used to scold me, man.'

– *That's the best way to learn.*

– *It helped me helluva lot.*

From the other side came a strident call: 'Sunny!' Sunny jumped to attention. 'Yes, boss! Wait, wait, bru, I'll serve my lahnee and I'll come back.'

By now you'd have gathered that the posh-talking Stranger was a first-time visitor to this neck of the woods and although it was pretty makeshift, as we had mentioned earlier, he was quite charmed by the cosiness it had somehow exuded, notwithstanding the Non-White Bar sign at the entrance, the wooden benches and the cracked enamel tables. Indeed he was so preoccupied with the attractions of this newfound watering hole that he hardly noticed the forlorn figure of a sugar worker, in well-worn blue overalls, his trademark working gear, ambling to the counter.

The figure seemed to be preoccupied with counting his small change. It was on the cards that at some point the Stranger would take more than a passing interest in the forlorn figure. Out of sheer politeness he avoided looking at him directly. Instead he absentmindedly watched him out of the corner of his eye. The forlorn figure did the same for him. The smaller the group of strangers, the more self-conscious people are. Such accidental intimacy breeds a sort of nakedness. Take two people in a lift. One farts, the whole world knows who did it.

The man in overalls needed a drink. That much was patently clear, but it seemed that from the way he counted and recounted his small change he might not have enough for a glass of cheap wine. Overalls turned half profile, yet still keenly glancing at the Stranger, who now could not hide a responding look. He was not given to reaching hasty conclusions but he detected a vague feeling of resentment in Overalls' body language, as if to say, 'If I want to drink wine, my bloody business!' However, what Overalls actually said to Sunny, just back from serving his lahnee, was, 'Sunny, give me glass wine.'

It was at this point that the Stranger saw that Overalls had a bright-eyed kid of about nine or ten in tow. Blithering Idiot No 1 was indignant. This was his domain and there were certain unwritten laws. If those laws were broken he turned into a small-time tyrant.

– *Hey, Mothie, you know you can't bring that fuller inside here!*

– *Hey, never mind, he not drinking, I'm drinking!*

– *I know, I know, but you know you can't bring that fuller here. Hey boy, stand by the door. You know what the lahnee will say, huh?*

– *Every time, lahnee, lahnee!*

– *Mothie, why this fuller never go school today?*

– *Big trouble by the house. Me too, I never go work today. I went police station to make one complaint.*

– *What complaint?*

– *I went there and they laugh at me.*

– *Don't be silly, they can't laugh at you.*

– *Those bloody bastards, man. They think they can act like that to me …*

'To ME.'

ME.

Mothielall Sewmungal, respected resident of Mount Edgecombe. Mothielall Sewmungal, father of six children. Mothielall Sewmungal, faithful employee of the Hulett Sugar Company for thirty years, never took one day off except when his mother died, giving his children a sound education, making sure his children were reared in age-old traditions and morals. 'To ME, Mothielall Sewmungal. Everybody knows ME in Mount Edgecombe. They think they can act like that to me and get away. You bloody see what I'm going to do today. I'll fix them up one by one! Yeah! Act like that to me and get away! You wait and see what I'm gonna do. Just wait and see.'

The Stranger found the man's forthrightness appealing. That's what was wanted – a healthy dose of indignation. That was a good way of moving forward; and a good thing for him, that's what people like Mothie should be looking to do – moving forward. Most of the time that wasn't the case and the Stranger knew it. Yet he looked for it in every forgotten corner, almost as a kind of vindication of his own dreams in a place which smothered dreams. He wasn't even conscious that he was always looking for it in people, and that he was doing so right now.

It only hit him that he was indeed staring, albeit in approval, when Mothie gave him that look – the look that said 'Who the ding-dong are you?' – as he checked his small change, which he took out of a knotted handkerchief. The Stranger had not been conscious that although his was a sideways glance, it was intense.

The old man scolded the little boy, 'Hey, monkey – don't come inside, man. You know that Uncle got nerves. You know he will shout. Come on, you stand by the door, I'm coming just now. Don't come inside, I'm coming just now.'

He spoke as if he was in his own house. The reference to his 'nerves' got Sunny going. 'Hey Mothie, what you saying I got nerves? You saw I got nerves?'

Mothie ignored him. 'Sunniya, nerves is nerves. Nev'mine, you my mart's laaitie. Give one glass wine.'

Sunny reached for the jar of Oom Tas red aperitif wine displayed on the counter behind him. The word aperitif was a posh word that covered many sins. Those in the know referred to the wine as rot-gut, made from proof or pure spirits diluted with cheap wine made from leftovers. You had to have a stomach made of cast iron to cope with it. Some believed Oom Tas was strong enough to corrode metal. As he poured out the wine he said indignantly, 'Mothie, you can't bring that fuller to the bar, you know you can't bring that fuller here.'

Mothie took a big sip, wiped his lips, again ignoring him. Sunny sighed and urged the wide-eyed youngster not to move from his position at the door. He needn't have worried. Prem was grateful for the privilege of being in this secret place where adults congregated, fascinated by the display of bottles behind the counter, bringing to mind the ditty he'd learnt in kindergarten – 'There were Ten Green Bottles hanging on the wall …' He fantasised about taking a pot shot with his rubber sling at the row of bottles, ' … one Green Bottle did accidentally fall / There'd be nine Green Bottles hanging on the wall.'

Mothie emptied the glass with another big swig and slammed it on the counter. 'Every time something new will come out for you, eh, Sunniya?' Sunny toned him down and reasoned, 'You know the lahnee will shout, man.'

By now Mothie should have appreciated the lahnee's right

to shout when he wanted to or when he was provoked. To Sunny that was a fact of life, like the sun rising in the east and setting in the west. Surely a man of Mothie's age and experience should know simple things like that? On the other hand this was not the way the old man usually behaved. As Sunny was to tell the Stranger later on – 'He doesn't come here every day, bru. When he comes he buys one two glasses of wine. Sits quietly in one corner and goes home early. His children come first. Something must be troubling him today.'

Mothie was not easily appeased. He made out that he didn't take too kindly to yes-men, and he believed that Sunny fell into this category with ease. Sunny was not anything like his father Kista as far as Mothie was concerned. Especially after several Oom Tas's he was always talking about how the younger generation didn't measure up. Another thing, they got carried away too easily. 'Hey, bugger your lahnee! Little bit position you get here, you think you own the place.'

Sunny ignored the jibe and offered Prem a cooldrink. 'Hey boy, come and take this lemonade and go.' Mothie urged his son, 'Go – Uncle giving mineral, go take.' Prem was delighted. It was not always that he was offered a cooldrink. On his way every day to and from school he passed an elevated hoarding on the main street in Mount Edgecombe displaying one of those eye-catching Coca-Cola signs with a huge bottle of ice-cold Coke in the hands of a beautiful, laughing girl. Whenever he came across that sign, his mouth drooled. No, not for the girl, you lecherous creep. At that age the Coke was far more appealing. But it was too expensive for him. He promised himself that when he grew up and started working he would buy himself an ice-cold bottle of Coke every day of his working life.

103

Sunny was puzzled. Why wasn't the kid at school? Mothie was strict about things like that and it was surprising to say the least. 'Why this fuller didn't go to school today?'

Mothie fairly exploded. 'Big trouble, man! Those bloody swines!'

Alarmed that such sonic abuse would upset the Boss, Sunny hushed him and pointed frantically to the White section. That made no difference. Whatever was troubling him was no trifling matter, especially now that the wine was slowly taking effect. His voice went up a few more decibels. Sunny pleaded, 'Sssh! Lahnee's next door, man.'

– Don't ssshush me, choothia!

Even being called an arsehole in Hindi didn't upset Sunny as much as what his lahnee's reaction would be. 'I told you lahnee's next door, man.'

– Hey, bugger your lahnee, man. I got my troubles here – lahnee, lahnee, lahnee!

This really got Sunny's goat. If it were someone else, he would have got the chingalan to throw him out. Nobody behaved like that in his domain, but he had a soft spot for the old guy. Mothie was a long-time family friend. Still, he couldn't behave as if this was his house, and he had to be brought into line. 'I told you one time, you won't listen, eh? I told you one time you won't bloody listen you, eh?'

Mothie, drowned in his own dilemma, didn't hear a word Sunny said. 'They think they can act like that to me. I'll fix them up today.'

Despite his annoyance, Sunny just had to know what was at the root of Mothie's distress. It must have been pretty serious for Mothie to have taken time off from work and taken his son out of school. He wanted to know who it was that Mothie was going to fix. 'Who you talking 'bout, Mothie?'

Mothie snarled again, not directly responding to the question. 'Those bastards, man. They think they can act like that to me and get away. You bloody see what I'm going to do today. I'll fix them up, one by one I'll fix them up! Yeah! You wait and see what I'm gonna do. Just wait and see. Hey Premwa, come here – you mustn't fright, huh. Tell them everything you saw. You tell them from the beginning what you saw. You mustn't be frightened. I'll be standing by you – right there. You go 'n stand by the door. They think they can act like that!'

– *What happened, why never go work today?*

– *I went there. I went there and they laugh at me, man. Police must look after us, not right, Sunniya?*

– *Yeah, right!*

– *How you'll like it if you go police station to make one complaint and they laugh at you? How you like that?*

'Hey, bru,' – he was talking to the Stranger too now, seeing he was being drawn into this unfolding drama with increasing fascination – 'where you heard story like that? You go police station to write your report and they laugh at you, where you heard story like that?'

The Stranger was not conscious of it but his smile was the smile of a man in a suit. The old man was upset that Sunny didn't take his word. 'Hey, Mai Keeriai, they laughing for nothing, man. Yeah, they don't know me yet. They don't know me yet. I'll tell my lahnee and I'll go straight by the magistrate.'

– *Hey, hey, hey! You can't go by the magistrate just like that.*

'I'll go, me. The police don't know me yet. They think they can laugh at me and get away. ME – Mothielall Sewmungal! You just wait and see what I'm going to do today.' Mothie

105

drained the glass. His mood softened a bit. 'Arreh, Sunniya, man! How long you know me, man?'

'I know you long time, Mothie.' Sunny turned to the Stranger and said, 'True, bru, I know him from when I was a laaitie.'

Mothie responded with equal warmth. 'Arreh, I know your whole family. I knew your father from the first day he started working barman here. 'You laaitie that time. I never used to drink those days, Sunniya. Never used to touch it, man. Hell, your father too – Kista – what a nice man! Arreh, what a good thunee player! We used to play partners.' They were an unbeatable team. 'When I say FORTY! Your father will look at the sky, which means, you go ahead, I got a strong hand. If he look down that means we shouldn't keep trump. If he touch his ears that means he's got Jack of Spades, his nose Jack of Diamonds, his eyes Jack of Clubs, his mouth Jack of Hearts. We knew all the tricks. Hell, your father too, man. What a nice man. Sorry he died, eh Sunniya?'

– *One of those things, man; got to die one day.*

'Yeah, where you can get man like that today? Work like a dog for his family. Where you can get man like that today?' Mothie paused, long enough for a quick glance at the Stranger, long enough to drive his point home. 'Little bit position they got, little bit edication they got, they think they somebody! Arreh, our time, man – our time. Saturday night! Jolling night. People coming from Durban, Sydenham all over. Full, full, Mount Edgecombe. Saturday night all night dancing! Wedding night! Your father, Mandraji fuller, right? And me, I'm Roti fuller. Arreh, but dancing time, we'll dance Natchannia together.'

– *What, my father too*?

'Yeah, I teach your father to dance. Arreh, chee! chee!

Sunniya, not like today's dancing. Everybody will go in one dark room – biting in the neck, putting tongue in the mouth. Or they'll put one fast music – then everybody …' Words failed him. He backed off from the counter and with the police forgotten he showed them how the Twist could be done. 'When this leg get tired – they'll put this leg. Hey, what about *that*, hey? And *that*?'

The Stranger, loosening up after his third double cane, felt his leg twitching to the beat. Sunny, no mean dancer himself, also found himself moving behind the counter to the rhythm, every now and then casting a glance over his shoulder just in case the lahnee showed up. 'Never, man, never!'

– *Arreh, our time, man, our time! Girls can't come out of the house – so strict they was. Arreh, six o'clock all the doors will be closed. Can't see one girl with one eyes. That time boys must dance girl's part. Saturday night! Saturday night! You know those big, big shots from Durban, Sunniya – arreh, all will come and sit in one place. Drinking whiskey, brandy, everything, man. You know your father will say, 'Put one number for them, put one number for the big, big shots.' Arreh, I'll say why you not starting the joll? But where that fuller want to start? Give him one two dops then that fuller on the tops. Your father! Me too, I'll hit the dholak – joll started!*

Mothie launched into a Natchannia song and spontaneously broke into the dance for it. He became louder, much to the consternation of Sunny, ever worried about what his lahnee would say. Sunny eventually stopped him just in time before the crescendo. Apologetic at having to cut across the nostalgia, Sunny was conciliatory. 'Lahnee's next door, man.'

'Bugger your lahnee, man.' Mothie paused, looked at his glass of wine, forgetting for a moment his current problems, and his visage broke into a distant, fond look of reminiscence of good times past. 'You remember that time, eh, Sunniya?' Sunny nodded. Mothie went on, with a dreamy smile. 'You laaitie that time. Hey, son.' Mothie waved a hand at Prem. 'Look my son. Clever fuller. Come out first every time in the school.'

They were disturbed by the lahnee's shout from the White section. 'Sunny!' Sunny jumped to attention but Mothie stopped him. 'Hey, Sunniya, wait, wait, wait! Give 'nother one wine quickly. Give 'nother one wine.'

The chemistry of unforced, spontaneous human communion had pulled them into a warmth which not even the lahnee's stentorian call could completely dispel. Sunny quickly poured out the wine and ventured, 'Hey, bloody good singer you was, eh?'

'That's nothing, listen this one.' Mothie promptly broke into 'Hey Ganga Maiya', an even louder tune. Sunny tried to hush him down as he left for the White bar. His departure put the final damper on the mood. With his song tapering off, Mothie turned to catch the Stranger gazing at him. He misread the look of appreciation. To Mothie, this was a man in a suit looking down at him.

Everything that had turned his ordered world into turmoil came to a flashpoint. Unfortunately, the Stranger was in the line of fire, an assault position born, it would seem, not only out of Mothie's present personal dilemmas but also out of the sullen, eternal resentment of those who feel unequal to others or have been made to feel that way.

So now, with Sunny gone, an awkward silence ensued. Mothie took his drink from the counter and walked to the table in a corner of the bar. He avoided the Stranger's eyes as he uttered with more than a little petulance. 'If I want to drink wine, my business.'

Suddenly and unexpectedly accosted thus, the Stranger, found himself feeling some guilt. He seemed an intruder in the old man's world. Much confused, he found himself on the defensive. His response emerged with an unintended gruffness, 'If you want to drink, man, drink. Why do you look at me when you say that?' The Stranger could sense, despite himself, that he was falling into a trap. Mothie felt the change in the balance. He was getting the better of the man in the suit and he toppled the first pawn with the words, 'I never looked at you.'

Again the unintended gruffness, this time even more so. 'Of course you looked at me. You looked at me and then you said that.'

It all made a sort of primal sense, not the usual kind of rationale he was used to, yet he could feel he was somehow losing his grip. Mothie pressed home the advantage – 'Answer me one thing. How you know I looked at you if you never looked me first?' He had his man. Wagging a finger at the Stranger, his voice rose in a note of triumph just as Sunny re-entered. 'Go 'n answer me that!' Mothie seemed to have flattened a somewhat embarrassed Stranger. He pressed on to the coup de grâce – 'Go 'n answer me that! You think you big shot because you drinking cane. Cane and wine same thing, man, you must get drunk.'

The Stranger's protestation was feeble: 'If you want to drink wine, that's your business, I didn't say anything.'

Mothie was in full cry. 'What you mean my business? Look, thumbi, I'm telling you nicely, I'm older than you – you got no respect?'

By the time Sunny, for the umpteenth time, had got back from serving his White customers, the Stranger had downed his fourth drink and Mothie his fourth glass of wine. The Stranger was counting, because two was his usual limit; but Mothie didn't hold with counting or limits. This was unusual for the Stranger. On the odd occasion he felt like a drink, his limit was two doubles. Sunny this time was determined to take matters in hand. Mothie was clearly overdoing it, troubling a respectable customer who was prepared to spend. He gently rebuked the old man. 'Mothie, he never do you nothing, why you troubling him?'

Despite the little power game there were indeed deeper considerations. For Mothie, although not a heavy drinker, there was no better place than a convivial pub to soothe the pain of everyday existence. For the Stranger, like Omar Khayyam, it provided space in which to mull over the many complexities and contradictions of life, a place to further mull over the eternal question:

WHAT THE DING-DONG IS LIFE ALL ABOUT?

For Mothie the hard grind and dull routine of existence was staple. Worrying about it wouldn't change things, would it? As he was to say to the Stranger much later, after the alcohol had again rendered a measure of cordiality, 'You worry, you die. You don't worry, you still die.' Then, following even more drinks, whether wittingly or unwittingly – it's left to you to judge – he posed the eternal question: 'Then why must die, bhai?' Which, perhaps, was another way of saying:

WHAT THE DING-DONG IS LIFE ALL ABOUT?

What indeed was it all about when the even tenor of his life was so disturbed that he was forced to enter the forbidding precincts of the Mount Edgecombe Police Station?

Sunny, returning at this point, was quick to size up what had happened and didn't want the Stranger upset too much. 'All right, leave it out, Mothie. Why you worrying him, he never do you nothing.'

– *You saw me making trouble in this bar, Sunny? How many years I'm coming here, you saw me making trouble?*

Doing his best to placate him, Sunny said gently, 'No, I never saw you making no trouble and all …'

– *Everybody knows me in Mount Edgecombe. I got lot respect. If I want to drink wine my bloody business. Why he must worry?*

Further appeasement from Sunny – 'But he never say nothing to you.'

– *How you know? – you wasn't here!*

Despite the awkwardness, the Stranger felt he had to add something. 'I didn't say a word.'

Mothi climbed in boots and all, exclaiming at his mimicking mocking best, 'I never say one word! You think because you drink cane, you big shot?'

This time Sunny was much firmer. 'Mothi, please, for God's sake, keep quiet!'

The old man bowed his head. He went back to his table in the corner, muttering, 'Whole day I got trouble. Nobody know my trouble. How much trouble I got.' The thought of his troubles set him off again. Raising his voice once more, he added, 'If I want to drink wine, I want to bloody drink wine!'

Casting a look backwards to the door in the partition, Sunny exclaimed, 'Sssh, man, don't make so much noise. The wit ous are laughing at us.'

Mothie grew even angrier. 'Let them laugh, hell! I'm

111

paying for my wine. Just because they white people I must start shivering for them.'

Sunny shouted despite himself. 'You making us a fool! You got no sense? You like white people must laugh at us? You got no shame?'

There was absolutely no stopping Mothie. 'What shame? You think I'm running naked here? This bar, this. Let them laugh. What, you think they God?'

It was futile, but Sunny still pleaded, 'Ssssh, man, I'm telling you nicely.'

The softer approach had some effect. 'Awright, awright. Gimme 'nother one wine. Wait, wait. I want to go lavatory. I'll go 'n make one piss and come back. Don't fight with me, Sunniya.'

– I'm not fighting. I'm only saying don't make so much noise.

As Mothie left he admonished his son, this time with the more outward display of affection that comes after a couple of glasses. 'Be careful, you stand by the door, monkey! Don't go inside, that Uncle will shout. I told you he got nerves. Awright, my sonnha, my jelebi?'

This sudden outpouring of fatherly affection touched both Sunny and the Stranger, who ventured after Mothie had left, 'He seems to be a good father.'

'Yeah, bru. He works hard. Doesn't come here every day. He just comes and have one two wine and goes home early. He gives his children everything. He got six children.' Sunny didn't add that Mothie's wife had died giving birth to their sixth child.

– Six children!

– Six children, bru.

– For God's sake, how does he manage?

– Poor people got all the trouble, bru. He only earns two pounds a week.

– Two pounds ...

– I don't know how he does it, but he sends them all to school.

It was all very true. Mothie's sudden loss of his wife meant he now also had to mother his kids. It was a tough time but thank God he was able to find employment as a tractor driver on the cane fields with the Hulett Sugar Company. He didn't earn much but the company gave him a house and his mother Banmathi had helped by turning their small patch of ground into a fairly good market garden, the produce from which she sold at a spot under the huge avocado tree on the side of the main road. And then life dealt him another blow when she died.

Mothie's misery at this second bereavement was leavened a bit when his lahnee gave him a loan to cover the expense of the thirteenth-day ceremony. And now, when he came back into the bar, mightily relieved and ready for another glass, and hearing Sunny talk of these matters from the past, he eagerly added a description of how the ceremony had gone. The thought occurred to the Stranger, as Mothie related the event, that moments like these tended to touch an almost invisible cord between the melanin-rich and the melanin-poor.

Yet could he really argue with the commissar of the underground cell he had joined when the man had said in ringing tones that such 'liberalism would not materially change the lives of people' – like Mothie, the Stranger now added to himself – 'as long as class interests along with colour dictated the distribution of wealth. Victory against capitalism is in the hands of the workers!'

So why didn't such people take hold of their lives? Made sense – the more you dropped your pants, the more you'd get dingged! If you didn't keep your belt tight you'd be inviting the dinggers of this world, and hell, there were lots of dinggers out there. He couldn't understand why people were prepared to put up with all that dingging. Even worse, they didn't dingg back! As the alcohol hit the button, the contradictions became even more acute. If something was wrong you had to put it right.

At the same time, the question also arose, was it not smarter, in the prevailing circumstances, to turn the other cheek like Sunny did with the traffic cop?

The Stranger didn't take too kindly to Sunny lying down and letting these guys walk all over him. But then he didn't have Sunny's perspective – that lying down had brought him immediate relief or reward depending on which way you looked at it, in that the cop didn't fine him. A fine would have bitten into his meagre resources which had to stretch to so many things, things like the rent, his kid's school fees, their clothing, the groceries and all that, things that most Ous tend to need whatever their employers may think.

The question that loomed larger for the Stranger was that if you weren't your own person, then

WHAT THE DING-DONG WAS LIFE ALL ABOUT?

There were times when you just had to stand up and say 'Shit!' That took some doing, some serious control. He believed he had been in control of his life except for that time when he met Shaik during his Varsity days.

Shaik was a fellow student. They were both very active in

the Students' Representative Council and had the chutzpah to say 'Shit!' quite often. The Stranger never forgot how Shaik roused the student body to action: 'Why are we here at Varsity? To get a degree to enable us to earn a living. Fine. And then what? To buy a nice house, nice car and have a nice family. That's fine also. It's what most students want to do in a normal society. But are we living in a normal society? Once we are out there earning a living what kind of world will we be living in? More importantly, what kind of world are we bequeathing to our children? Mahatma Gandhi argued for passive resistance – but there's action action too. The workers are marching, the women are marching. And what are we doing? Search your conscience – what are we doing?'

That speech shocked him. Such was his performance that Shaik came across as a man of conviction, fearless and willing to take on the most menial of tasks in the course of bucking the system. Both were on the verge of being kicked out but somehow they had managed to graduate. The celebrations had to be something special, but all of them were flat broke. Shaik had showed his usual resourcefulness. He used his activist credentials to inveigle some Grey Street businessmen into parting with a contribution to the Struggle.

Up to that point in his life, the Stranger was sure he was in control of things, except, of course, for the jerking in his youth. Together with Shaik, he'd joined an underground resistance cell. By God, he was determined to change things.

He didn't realise that the movement demanded complete discipline and that a cadre's every move was under scrutiny. He had always valued his independence, never part of the herd. Soon, however, the feeling among the hierarchy was that he liked his dop a little too much. He conceded that he enjoyed a beer or two but he was convinced that he was as disciplined as the next cadre. The others were not so sure, especially Comrade Shaik. When it came out that Shaik was the one who had ratted on him, he wondered why such a brave, committed soul would stoop so low. He dismissed a suggestion from one of his mates that Shaik saw him as a threat to his leadership aspirations. That way he was naïve, as later events were to prove. He stuck to the view that Shaik was that much-vaunted creature, a disciplined cadre.

He slowly found himself relegated to the margins of the cell, but that did not stop the fire burning within. Not so long ago he would have gone straight to the bathroom and jerked off his frustration. Nature in due course imposes limits to self-gratification. With gradual maturity the thrill pales before the real thing. In fairness, let us recall that even before the onset of such maturity he had made that huge decision, one of the major achievements in his life, to shake off the shaking. Initially it took much lower-lip biting but after an almighty struggle at the age of sixteen, instead of locking himself in the bathroom he took his dog for a run in the wooded hills near his house. He ran around in the soft red sands, dodging aged mango trees, every now and then throwing punches like an imaginary Rocky Marciano, till he was panting as much as his dog. He eventually did it. No more jerking!

Talk about discipline! If the hierarchy had only known just how much discipline it took to jettison his phallocentric inclinations and in breaking off a very promising relationship, they would never have doubted his fervour for the cause. His steely will in sticking to the principles of the Struggle would have been gloriously affirmed.

Discipline!

But for discipline, he might still have been hitting it off with the sensuous Hawa Bibi Majumdar.

It was evident from the start. He sat on the low wall outside what passed for the student carfeteria at the 'tribal' college, the make-shift Indian University on Salisbury Island, sipping from a can of Coke. He wasn't particularly thirsty. That's what students did when they were kicking their heels – drank Coke, although the more adventurous dashed it with some interesting spirituous liquids. But, for what seemed a fleeting glance, they did not look directly at each other in that breathless first encounter.

Total strangers in a constant student tidal wave, something clicked reminding him of the song, 'Some enchanted evening, you may see a stranger / Across the crowded room …'

Wordlessly she sat right next to him, looking straight ahead. Lingering moments later she crept a little closer. He noticed but couldn't believe his luck. Except that it wasn't evening and it wasn't a room, but it was crowded and they were strangers. He smiled. She didn't, but the glint in her eye gave her away.

She said without looking at him,

'You look like you're starving.'

'Beg your pardon?'

'Cut the crap, you'd like to have it, wouldn't you?'

She spoke looking straight ahead and nobody would have guessed that such a loaded conversation was ensuing.

Startled, he could barely whisper, 'What?'

The deadpan look gave way to a slight quiver of the lips, a lift of the cheek muscles, suggesting the faintest of smiles. She didn't answer the question. Instead she looked at him directly for the first time. She asked, 'What's your name?'

He replied, 'What's yours?'

The answer came in a flash, 'Hawa.' It sounded like the old fashioned Baboo-English version of 'Here you are.'

He said, 'I'll take it.'

Before she could counter, he added, 'What happened to your hijab?'

And they both cracked up. They didn't need much convincing that it was this thing about first sight that they make so much of in pulp fiction. Unlike starry-eyed lovers in pulp fiction, instant chemistry was accompanied by instant communication and there was no need for sweet, self-conscious nothings.

Hawa did not have the finely chiselled features or the doe-eyes of the sirens of Indian cinema. Neither did she have their olive complexion touched every so often by those faint, fleeting flushes of innocence triggered by long-distance Bollywood song and dance routines. It had often occurred to her that this formulaic posturing was packaged as 'family entertainment' although they strongly resembled the mating dances of the feathered species, particularly of cocks of exotic plummage. The dance routines went further, even more explicitly executing the crotchet thrust than its innovator, Michael Jackson had done. None of those coy peeks from behind the purdah for Hawa Bibi Majumdar.

Yes there was a difference about her and he said to himself, 'Viva la difference!' One of his language courses was French.

To begin with, Miss Difference didn't hide behind a purdah because she didn't wear one. She refused to wear one. Her mother threw a fit. In fact, she almost threw Hawa out of the house, and she would have, if her father hadn't put his foot down. Her old man was ambivalent. In truth it didn't matter one way or the other to him. During their heated exchange, she ranted, 'You so stupid that's why you working in a government hospital. That's why we staying in

Chatsworth. If you was like Dr. Moosa Mohideen, with his own private hospital, we would be staying in La Lucia under permit. But no! You the saint!' In full throttle she quoted an old Urdu saying, 'If you haven't got money your own dog won't bite you!' The way she understood her religion, dogs were taboo, they were lowly creatures, not fit to be kept as pets or even watch-dogs. If such a lowly creature thought you were so lowly that it wouldn't even deign to bite you, then how low must you be! And with that she threatened to leave home.

Abdul Aziz was a good man, but he was also a man. For one blinking moment he was tempted to call her bluff and the thought struck him – great, now I can do more than smile at that beautiful young staff nurse who has given me the come-on more than once. But he was a good man, although he wished he wasn't a good man, especially when his wife, with a virtual tyre of cellulite around her waist, shuffled into bed alongside him, grunting at every move. By everything that was holy, how he wished he wasn't a good man.

If Hawa had her way she would have changed her first name. She would, however, have stoutly resisted any suggestion of so jettisoning her surname. Her father had given her every reason to be proud of him. Adul Aziz Majumdar was more concerned as a medical man with kwashiorkor and stuff like that which he witnessed in abundance in the government hospital he worked at. His version of his religion was that it was more concerned with stuff like that than with stuff like the purdah.

When she was still green behind the ears she heard her father chiding his mother for doing things like serving tea to the servant in a broken cup. Her father would say, 'They are people too. You must treat them like you treat us.'

At that stage she wondered how her father could be so stupid. These people were certainly not like us. How could they drink from the same cup? As she grew up, however, she also grew up to appreciate that drinking from a different cup was more an indication of idiocy than of intelligence.

When, at high school, she got into trouble for the umpteenth time, unlike most of the other parents her father had stood by her. She had a knack for getting into trouble. She had once got into trouble by standing up to her principal. The principal, Mrs. Parimala Pillai, on the urging, no doubt, of her husband, Mr. Pook Pillai, had invited Mangope, the president of Bophuthatswana, another of those Bantustans with which the Wit Ous thought they could pull the wool over people's eyes. A few like Mangope lapped up the mess of pottage that were thrown down to them for their arse-licking. So too did Pook who had developed such a fondness for messes of pottage that his tongue hung out at every possible opportunity.

How could one not be proud of a father who took on the Special Branch of the SA Police urgently summoned by Pook the moment he saw the first placard being waved by Hawa and her small, rag-tag, pimply, pig-tailed army.

Hawa Bibi Majumdar was not given to impulsive decisions but the moment she had encountered the Stranger, their intimacy was so immediate that she had not taken umbrage at the joke about her name. It was a corny old joke that did the rounds of male students who thought they were men simply because they could crack corny old jokes like that. The joke about the name Hawa sprang out of the patois mangling of "here you are!" Thus "hawa" was regarded as what any respectable call-girl would say to a customer as she got under the sheets.

Hawa had an allure of another kind. Despite her mother's fulminations, she did not wear a bra. Firm breasts did slight seductive jiggles beneath the plain, discreetly translucent tops she generally wore. Sure this knocked him out everytime but what was just as seductive was her bluntness. It was the bluntness of one who didn't kid herself about anything. As she did in her classes, she got right down to it, saying it like it was.

At first her directness to a complete stranger, especially about his 'wanting it' niggled him. Did she flaunt herself with all the boys like this? As it turned out he had to confess, for all his liberality about sex, that he was somewhat relieved when he found that she was certainly no easy catch. Before their first coital conjugation, it came down to what they both denied, him more than her, that it was plainly and simply the primeval ritual of the hunt.

Oh yes, she was candid about her sexuality and they had huge giggles when they eventually confided their masturbation secrets. She surprised him with her maturity. She said, 'Did you know that masturbation is quite normal with monkeys?'

He was no mean slouch when it came to useless information, but confessed that he didn't know this one. She retorted in that smart-assed way she sometimes did, 'Had a strange feeling you were no monkey.'

He let that one pass and necked her quite openly in the student common room much to the disgust of both the members of the Hindu Youth Brigade and the Young Warriors of The Final Prophecy. She whispered in his ears when she noticed a heavily bearded, heavily bespectacled young man in the far corner staring at them, 'Don't look now but I think the commander of the local God Squad is not pleased with our unbridled demonstration of deep affection.' He whispered back, 'Perhaps I should complete his enjoyment by taking my pants off – I actually have a strong urge to do just that.'

So how did this match which seemed to have been made in heaven come to an end?

Discipline.

The unwritten law of underground resistance was that emotional entanglements were millstones that had to be jettisoned. It didn't end the way it usually did in an Amitabh Bachen movie – loads of violins in the background. They were quite sensible about it – he drank himself into a stupor and she wore a veil to hide her swollen eyes, which pleased her mother no end.

Disicipline!

He was utterly convinced that he had what it took. How could he foresee that the time would come when that conviction would be put to the test? Was it fate or was it another of those inexplicable accidents? Or was it due, heaven forbid, to something else he had no say in? Was it due to the fact that he was what some believed was an endangered species, a Char Ou?

Chapter Two

It was now around two pm. It occurred to the Stranger that he had spent more time than he had intended at the White House Hotel. He had happened on the hotel while he was looking for an address – he had to deliver a parcel from his company on his way back from taking orders at retail outlets on the North Coast.

But gravitating to a bar was not pure accident either. He was by way of being a frustrated member of his generation. The rot had started long ago, when things had caught up with him and he was unceremoniously expelled from Varsity. He should have listened to his father and completed his studies before attempting to solve the problems of the world, as the old man put it. He hadn't even heeded his advice to lose the posters of Che Guevara and the Free Mandela Campaign. The old man was saved from further anxieties in this case, it seems, by the kindly hand of fate when he was quietly summoned in his sleep into the Great Beyond. Everyone said it was a very peaceful passing, as if that mattered one way or the other. As the Stranger saw it, in his uncluttered way, the point was that if you went, you went. Full stop. At any rate, after the old man had ditched his mortal frame the Stranger not only put the posters back on his wall, he also stepped up his activism by several gears.

Now, however, whenever he had a hard time trying to convince a customer to buy his wares, he found himself cooling off from his commitment to justice just that little bit and reluctantly he had to agree that the old man had been prescient. He hated the banality of salesmanship. If it hadn't been for his activism he would have finished his law studies and become a successful lawyer like some of his colleagues who had, unlike him, kept their mouths shut and finished their studies. Now that they were firmly ensconced in plush offices they made one or two politically credible noises, as part of their good business sense.

He was fortunate to find a job as a salesman for a stationery company. If you were blacklisted it was difficult to get a job, but he had bluffed his way in, beginning as a footslogging salesman going from shop to shop in the Durban area and a little beyond. He had done so well that the company soon gave him a company car and a sales route that included the greater Durban area and much of the North Coast. That day he had to deliver a parcel to a school principal. As he drove through the main road, his attention was arrested by the White House Hotel standing so majestically alongside the road among huge trees, banana and sisal shrubs in a break in the cane fields that dominated either side of the road.

For the past few days he had put in long hours. He was working towards the point when he would own his own stationery shop, and he didn't mind pushing himself. Right now, however, he was having a much-needed break. Also, the heat was Very Hot and perhaps he would treat himself to a drink or two. As we have indicated, he was quite charmed by the pub and as we have also seen it soon got to more than a drink or three, or four. Let's not jump the bottle, OK?

While Mothie visited the toilet again, the attention of

the Stranger and Sunny shifted to the little boy Prem, who by now had shot down well over a hundred Green Bottles. Sunny called to the youngster. 'Come here, boy, bring the bottle. Why didn't you go to school today?'

The youngster handed Sunny the bottle. 'My father stopped me.'

– *What standard you?*

– *Standard One.*

– *Yes, eh, what you came out in your exams?*

– *First!*

– *Clever boy, huh! What you going to be when you grow big?*

– *I don't know.*

Sunny proffered some advice. 'What you mean you don't know? You must become a doctor or lawyer. You must make a big man of yourself.'

The Stranger, looking on with great curiosity, felt compelled to enquire, 'Tell me, boy, why did your father stop you from school today?'

Prem hesitated. Sunny urged him on. Prem began, 'You know my sister, she was in …'

In the interests of keeping up the suspense, we have written in Mothie's return from the toilet at this crucial moment, preventing Prem from divulging what should be a mouth-watering little mystery. When he saw the little boy inside the bar having a right royal conversation with Sunny and the Stranger he yelled at his son, 'Hey, what you standing there? Told you, you must stand by the door. Go outside now! Hey Sunny, what you making kooser-kooser with my son?'

Embarrassed at being caught inveigling the little boy into telling them what went wrong in his household to necessitate his absence from school and his father's visit to the police station, Sunny meekly replied, 'He only brought the bottle here, man.'

Mothie was not to be fooled. 'I know you. Give me my wine now.'

As we have already indicated it was unusual for Mothie to be imbibing so much wine. Sunny reasoned, 'Daytime now, Mothie …'

Mothie was indignant. 'I know it's daytime. I can see it's daytime. Why you telling me it's daytime? You think I'm stupid?'

– *I didn't say you stupid.*

– *You clever fullers, all you fullers, man. You think I'm stupid because I'm a tractor driver. You just like the police fullers.*

– *I didn't say you stupid. I said daytime now, why you drinking so much?*

– *Hey, you are not giving me free drink. If I want to drink, my business!*

This was getting out of hand for Sunny, ever conscious of the reaction from the other side of the partition. 'Don't shout, man.'

– *Why you stopping me from drinking then?*

The cork shot out of Sunny's bottle completely and he fairly exploded, 'I'm not bloody stopping you! For God's sake, I'm only trying to tell you …'

At that precise moment he was stopped in full cry by another stentorian shout from the lahnee – 'Sunny!'

Even at the height of his anger, Sunny never forgot his place in the grander scheme of things. With instant dexterity he was again the obsequious vassal –

– *Yes, boss!*

Life's transience is never more evident than in such rapid shifts in human behaviour. Mothie took full advantage of this absurdity by mimicking Sunny's response –

– *Yes, boss!*

The Stranger found it hard not to laugh out loud. The old man continued in a burst of new friendliness towards him, 'Too much frightened fuller, bhai. Not like his father, Kista. Me, I don't fright for my lahnee. My lahnee likes me. You know how long I'm working for him, bhai?'

– *Tell me …*

– *Thirty years!*

– *In the same job?*

– *One job, one boss!*

The tension abated. Taking pity on the troubled old man, the Stranger was apologetic. 'Uncle, I'm sorry about that little argument we had just now.'

It was at this juncture that Mothie advanced his homespun, somewhat surprisingly existential take on life that we mentioned earlier: 'Arreh, jaanethe bhai. Little, little thing like this we worry about, when we die what we take with us? When you worry, you die, when you don't worry you still die. Then why must die, bhai?'

They paused in companionable silence to ponder this together. 'Yes, bhai,' Mothie went on. 'Thirty years I'm working for my lahnee.' And he told the Stranger just how good his lahnee had been to him by lending him money to observe the thirteenth-day religious ceremony after his mother died. 'Where I must get so much money? I mean, I'm the eldest, my job to do the ceremony. Cost lot of money – all the connections and people from the district must be invited – lot of money for the tent, for the food and the pundit. Where I must get so much money? Then I asked my lahnee. He

127

never say nothing, didn't even ask me why I want the money. He just put his hand in his back pocket and took out so much notes. Bhai, white people carry so much money, eh?'

Sunny, back from serving the lahnee, caught the rest of the conversation and Mothie's conciliatory mood as he continued, 'Up till today he never ask me for the money. Where can you get lahnee like that? But this fuller, I don't know. Mustn't fright for your lahnee, Sunniya.'

'I'm not frightened.' Sunny glanced at them both. 'Who says I'm frightened for my lahnee?'

Mothie, with the obvious approval of the Stranger, went on giving advice. 'You mustn't fright. You must just do your work. Your lahnee can do you fuckall.'

– *Sssh, man. I think you better go home. How long your son is waiting for you? He must be hungry. You better take him and go home.*

– *Sunniya, haven't got your mother's vade to sell?*

– *No, only afternoon time, vade must be sold fresh otherwise not nice...*

– *Yeah, you right, so tasty when it's fresh, no?*

And thinking of food, Mothie sent his son off with money for bread, telling him there was some brinjal curry, and probably a little of the chicken curry left over from the evening before. After he left Mothie added with some pride, 'Clever fuller, Sunny. He come out first every time in school.'

The Stranger said, 'You must not stop him from school like this, Uncle. He seems an intelligent child. He must go to school every day, then one day he will go to high school, and then maybe to university and then who knows ...'

They waited for Mothie to reply. Suddenly he looked close to tears. 'I want to do so much for my children, bhai, I don't want they must battle like me, I work hard, bhai – Sunny, you know for yourself. Five o'clock, bhai, five o'clock I'm on that tractor. I want to do so much for my children.'

'Hey, bru, is true what you say.' Sunny came round the corner of the counter and put a friendly hand on Mothie's shoulder. 'You go home, have a rest, come back later.'

Mothie struggled to speak. 'I don't want to go home, Sunny. If I go home I'll only sit down and cry. My boy, Prem, he saw it, Sunny, he saw it –'

In between sobs the old man spoke of the shame that was visited on his family without warning. 'Disgrace. I tell you, Sunny, it's a disgrace for us. First time thing like this happened in our family. My boy, Prem, he's clever fuller. Every time I go home, first thing I ask for is my boy. He listen so nice to me. Yesterday he's hiding. I washed and all, and I thought funny, where's my boy. I call him, he's crying. I say, "Son, why you crying?"'

That's how they heard the story. Prem had come home from school which was just down the road from his house during the interval to fetch his homework book. He tried the front door but it was locked. Then he then went in through the back door, which was unlatched. His eldest sister who was around fifteen and who had been stopped from school to prepare her for marriage, was nowhere in sight. Then he heard strange sounds coming from the bedroom. He tiptoed to the room and – 'He saw my daughter, Sunny, he saw my daughter. She was sleeping with one man!'

Mothielall Sewmungal, tractor driver for the Hulett Sugar Company for thirty years, who never took one day off, eldest son of Sewmungal from Uttar Pradesh, proud father of six well-bred children, could not contain his outrage, his deep grief. It was not in him to see that nature sometimes took a detour from the straight and the narrow.

His humiliation poured out in starts of words and tears. 'How you like that? Since my wife died, I bring her up like one gold. I give my children everything. Look my position. I don't buy for myself. I give my children everything. I want my children must marry nicely, not like this. Every penny I get I put one side, that one day word will come for her and I'll marry and I'll give it. Now she gone do a thing like to me … To ME.'

Mothie's reaction was time-honoured. If discipline couldn't come from inside, it had to come from outside. From the wellsprings of his moral outrage and perhaps from a kind of love that conformity springs from, Mothielall's only recourse was violence.

He didn't say what he did, only that his daughter fled. 'She ran away … she ran away … now I don't know where she's gone.' And with that, Mothie Sewmungal broke down completely.

Chapter Three

Sunny and the Stranger could but offer one or two words of comfort, their reaction being totally different from that of the cops at the Mount Edgecombe Police Station. What both were certain of was that they had to help, to reach out to this old man. The Stranger felt that he also had to reach out to the young lady, how he just didn't know at the time. He had always felt a kind of ambivalence about 'discipline', the leit motif of the country's obsession with its melanin-influenced brand of Law and Order and of the tradition from which the likes of Mothie emerged.

After the storm of his emotions the old man asked for another glass of wine. This time Sunny was quick to pour it out but Mothie said, 'Wait, wait, wait. I go 'n wash my face and come. Same time I go 'n make one piss and come.'

After he had gone, Sunny and the Stranger sat in silence for a while before the Stranger started speaking almost mechanically, saying things which he knew didn't come completely from the heart, things perhaps which people like Sunny expected to hear –

– *Kids nowadays cause a lot of problems.*

– *True's God. You know, when we was laaities we couldn't catch a joll like today's laaities. We used to get it – one day my father hit me with a sjambok.*

– Today they've got the free life. Even the teachers can't hit them. What's the good of that? We used to get six of the best if we didn't learn our lessons. Today, I'm not sorry …

Even as he spoke the Stranger was not quite sure that he was being completely sincere, but there are times when, as creatures of habit, we carry on speaking nonetheless. Sunny's instant agreement had greater immediacy; for was that not what life was all about for him, immediacy? 'Me too! That day when my father hit me with a sjambok, I wanted to pull out of the house.'

The mood was right for reminiscence. At such times, little excuse is needed for harking back to the good old days, for heart-warming, if not much embroidered, flashbacks. Sunny went back to his early teens when he and his buddies were caught pinching mandarins from Bullwa's Farm, famous in the area for its rows of mandarin trees loaded with delicious fruit. It was well known also because Bullwa the owner chose to sell his fruit in the English Market rather than the Indian Market. Smart move – the Wit Ous had money. Of course, Sunny got belted by his old man. 'My father took the sjambok. One thing he didn't like, stealing. Hell, he gave it to me. Nowadays the laaities don't catch it like that.'

As you can guess, the Stranger agreed emphatically. Yet deep down there was an unease. All his life he had shrunk a little in the face of violence, which is not to say that he didn't bang his fist on the bonnet of his car when it refused to start on a cold day.

The small talk continued. The Stranger observed that the Bullwas of this world were a dying breed, and there many like him in Mayville, the upper-class side of Cato Manor where he was born and grew up. Sunny agreed enthusiastically – he remembered Cato Manor before 'the Wit Ous kicked us out'. Sunny fondly recalled the family's visits to his uncle in Blinkbonnie Road. 'We used to go there for porridge prayers.'

– *Blinkbonnie Road? What's your uncle's name?*

– *Nagan.*

'Nagan?' The Stranger had a feeling he knew Sunny's uncle. 'His name sounds very familiar.'

– *Wait, wait. You know Surprise Laundry?*

– *Yes.*

– *There by the bioscope?*

– *Yes, yes!*

– *Well, my uncle was married to Surprise Laundry's daughter.*

That remark was the clincher for the Stranger. Nagan was one of those Cato Manor residents who got on with everybody, especially the kids – and the Stranger was one of them. He and Sunny found it sensible to have another round at this point, and further fond memories emerged.

– *You-all had a big place there, bru?*

The Stranger recalled the shenanigans of the Department of Community Development, a generous euphemism for what was, in effect, The Largest Estate Agency in the World. The Stranger would have preferred to call it The Most Crooked Estate Agency in the World.

He described how the family had built their home with their own hands, working over weekends and any spare time. In the name of Community Development they were kicked out, paid peanuts and sent to the matchbox homes of unserviced Indian, coloured and African townships.

Sunny observed that the melanin-challenged could do anything and get away with it. The Stranger knew it would not make any difference to Sunny but he sang his pet lament anyway: 'The trouble is we let them get away with it.'

– *Yes, Sunny. You know, we built that house ourselves. My father was a baker's driver and he earned very little, but he always had this dream that he would one day build his own house. From the little he was paid he was able to buy building materials whenever he could, and all of us pitched in; afternoons, weekends. It took a long time but eventually we built it. Our own house! We lived there so happily until the whites came and kicked us out.*

– *What, they gave you-all lot money, bru?*

– *A lot of money, hell! They paid us peanuts – and now I'll bet they'll sell the same place for ten times the price.*

– *Yeah, the wit ous can do anything and they can get away with it.*

– *The trouble is we let them get away with it.*

'What can you do, bru? You say anything, you gone! Me, when my lahnee say anything I keep quiet. My job comes first. When I want anything from a wit ou I say 'Sir'. They get very happy when you call them Sir.' All of which reminded Sunny of the cop who called him a bliksem and how the word Sir had saved the day. Survival tactics be damned,' said the Stranger. Like Mothie, he was all for putting dignity first.

Sunny's reaction was true to form: 'Yeah, but sometimes it pays to act stupid. What you going to get by arguing? Look how many fullers they put in jail for saying something about the white people. They put you in jail for nothing. They come and take you away in the night. What they call that when they take you away?'

– *You mean they detain you.*

– *Something like that. If they detain me, who's going to buy bread for my kids, tell me that.*

– *All of us don't think like that.*

– *Wait, wait, answer me that. When they detain you, who's going to pay the rent and buy the children's food and all. Who's going to do that?*

This was getting tiresome for the Stranger. Here he was trying to make him see things as they were but Sunny just wasn't listening. What was worse was that he was being badgered with an overdose of Sunny's kiss-arse rationale. Thankfully Mothie, returning from the toilet, exploded, 'Arreh, chee! chee! I went there to make piss but number two came out. The lavatory stinking. Better tell your lahnee to get us better lavatory. Every day we come and spend our money and they give us stinking lavatory.'

– *I don't know how many times I told my lahnee.*

Mothie didn't swallow that. 'Don't bluff, you never tell him. You frightened fuller you.'

– *Oh shut up, Mothie man – why I must fright to tell him thing like that? But some of our fullers too, man, they terrible, they mess the lavatory up.*

– *Hell, got one bucket there …*

The Stranger was aghast – 'One bucket for all of you?'

Mothie was in full stride. 'One bucket! Everybody must use. What you expect, must get full up. I feel sorry for the fuller who must carry it. Haven't got one chain lavatory like the white fullers got.'

– *What you mean, chain lavatory?*

– *When you pull the chain, you silly fuller, the water comes out and all the shit gets washed away.*

Sunny was determined to put Mothie in his place. High on his horse, he asked, 'You got chain lavatory by your house?'

– *No, but …*

Sunny pursued his quarry, 'Have you got it, yes or no?'

– *No, but you see …*

– No buts. If you got bucket lavatory by your house, you must keep it clean, right? Then why you can't keep it clean here?

Mothie was well up on his lavatorial logic. 'Hey, my house not bar. Lot, lot people don't use my bucket. My bucket don't get full up. You talking shit, man. And the place where you make piss too – there they haven't got water coming out from the pipe like automatic.'

– Like what?

– Like it's automatic, man – it works on its own, like automatic car.

It suddenly occurred to Mothie that they were taking the mickey out of him and he shouted, 'Hey what, you think I'm stupid? You think I never go to school?'

– Awright, don't shout, I told you the lahnee's next door.

Mothie pounced. 'You must tell your lahnee next time he want to make shit, he must make shit in our lavatory and then you see how he like it. He'll never go there.' Of course, Mothie was not to know that the lahnee was in so much of shit right now in his personal life that it wouldn't matter which toilet he went to.

The Stranger heartily agreed with Mothie, 'He most certainly won't go there, Uncle.'

Sunny struggled to put across the eternal truth that there were always two sides to a story. As far as he was concerned, patrons also had a responsibility. Gently he protested, 'But some of our fullers too, man.'

Mothie was outraged. 'Hey, what you mean, "Some of our fullers too, man"? What, you think we dirty people, what? Our girls don't use scent and … what that thing they put here?'

The Stranger helped him out. 'Deodorant, Uncle.'

Mothie was in full cry. 'Yeah, same thing. Our girls don't use all that. You know why? They must bath every day in running water when they light the God lamp. They don't eat beef and pork. Our girls don't smell like the white girls.'

The smile on the face of the Stranger came out of hiding as Mothie reasoned, in his own way, that all people smelt if they did not have the luxury of daily baths, among other sound and more affordable ablutionary habits. Mothie was also emphatic that upbringing was all-important. Which took him on to talk about how he reared his children:

– Yeah, bhai, me I taught my daughter so nicely. When her mother died I brought her up like one gold. Not easy to bring up a girl, you know that. My sister said she must come and stay with her. I don't know why I never send her. You know me, Sunny, I'm very independent fuller. I said I'll bring her up myself, I'll bring her up myself. Gimme 'nother one wine Sunny!

– No, no more, Mothie. You've had enough.

– Gimme 'nother bloody wine, man!

– Awright, don't shout.

– Wait, wait. I got no more money left.

The Stranger, now completely taken by the old man's plight, offered to pay for the drinks. But Mothie was a proud man still conscious that this was a man in a suit. He protested, 'You rich fuller, huh – I'm not a beggar.'

The Stranger persisted until Mothie said Yes. A measure of conviviality having returned, the Stranger also offered to find the culprit who had so invaded this once tight little family. Mention of the incident again roused the old man's ire: 'If I catch him, I'll kill him with my bare hands. They don't know me yet. The polices don't know me yet. They laugh at me. What they think? I'm going by his house and I'm going to hit him in his own house.'

Sunny, who knew practically everybody in Mount Edgecombe, was impatient to know who the culprit was. 'What's his name?'

Ignoring Sunny's question, Mothie powered on. 'I'll hit him in his own house. What they think! They don't know me yet. You ask anyone here in Mount Edgecombe, bhai. Go outside and ask. Ask them about Mothie. I don't look for trouble. I mind my own business, but when anyone make trouble for me, hell!'

Sunny persisted, 'Who's this chap, man?

Mothie wasn't listening. 'Last time by the working place I hit one fuller …'

This was too much for Sunny. 'There we go again, number one story teller!'

But Mothie just went on talking to his avid listener, the Stranger. 'I hit this fuller, bhai. You know what he did? This fuller go 'n burn me to the lahnee. Arreh, he go 'n tell the lahnee I'm ducking and going home lunchtime. For nothing. Jealous fuller. You know, the lahnee likes me. I hit him one shot in front of the lahnee. He fell down like one cut fowl. I told him prove it. He didn't know what to say. The lahnee started laughing. He say, "Awright Mothie, leave him, I believe you." So good name I got in Mount Edgecombe. What you think I must keep quiet now?'

Sunny was persistent too. 'But who's this chap interfering with your daughter, man?'

– *You know Boywa?*

– *Which Boywa?*

– *Boywa Singh – that fuller fell down from the tree.*

'Oh, that Boywa!' Sunny turned to the Stranger. 'Hey, helluva thing happened in Mount Edgecombe. The spook

138

killed him. That's the strangest thing ever happened in Mount Edgecombe.'

You could see the Stranger was enthralled. Sunny jostled to tell the story but Mothie was in full flight. 'Up to today they don't know how that thing happened. There's a spook in that tree. I tell all the children, twelve o'clock time don't go by the tree – but where they'll listen?'

In the bar's alcoholic cosiness an uncanny urban legend unfolded. On the stroke of midnight Boywa, moving like a zombie, suddenly started to climb the gum tree alongside the main road. No one could stop him. Halfway up, he started to sing. 'We shouted, "Hey, Boywa, come down, man."' Mothie paused, relishing the timing. 'This fuller started climbing again. He got to the top, the branch got broken, Boywa fell down, broke his neck and died! Same Boywa Singh!'

Sunny was astonished, 'Not Boywa's son?!'

– *No, his connection. They too live in Verulam. He got one maroon Anglia car.*

– *You actually saw this fuller interfering with your daughter?*

– *No, but my son saw him.*

– *How you know he's Boywa's connection?*

– *Hell, you think I'm stupid? My son saw him at Boywa's house one day.*

– *You mad, man! Just because he was there that means he's Boywa's connection? What's his name?*

– *Johnny.*

– *Johnny? He got long hair? Got one smart car?*

– *Same fuller! Don't know about the smart car, but he got long hair. You know him?*

It occurred to Sunny that it might not be prudent to divulge much more. 'You know what you do? You go to the police station and lay your complaint now before you get too drunk. Otherwise they'll lock you up.'

This upset Mothie even more. 'That will be the day! They must just lock me and you'll see. I'll go straight to the magistrate, me ...' The old man stoutly refused to heed the pleas of the Stranger and Sunny to stop drinking for now and go to the police.

None of them saw the lahnee come in, certainly not the Stranger as he said, 'I think that's a good idea – you can come back after that. The important thing is to find your daughter.'

The lahnee, catching up with the conversation, agreed with the Stranger, and with his consonants particularly pointed and his vowels particularly rounded despite a slight slur in his speech, he commanded Mothie, 'That's right my friend – you'd better go to the police. See Sergeant Labuschagne. Tell him I sent you.'

Despite his distress, Mothie seemed somewhat pleased that the lahnee was taking an interest in his problems. 'You know my troubles, boss?'

'Yes,' said the lahnee, 'I heard it loud and clear. You Indians certainly know how to use your vocal chords.'

The police had laughed at him, Mothie complained. Which police?, the lahnee wanted to know. One Indian and one African policeman, Mothie told him. 'Police must take complaint, they mustn't laugh, not right, boss?'

'Naturally.' He had to agree, but the lahnee couldn't let the side down. 'Well, the way you're carrying on, snot and tears all over the bloody floor, they must have laughed at you. They were just having a little fun, I suppose. They won't laugh this time. You go and see Sergeant Labuschagne.'

The lahnee had spoken and Mothie would do his bidding

but he needed another drink first ('Sure, boss, I'll have one more drink and I'll go'). The boss was adamant and Mothie left right away. The lahnee glared at Sunny, 'Christ, what the hell do you people think this is, the Indian Market?'

As he also left, Sunny looked smugly at the Stranger. 'You see, if you're nice to a white man, you see how they'll help you out?'

The Stranger had difficulty keeping down the bile. 'Yes, I suppose that's true if you're a good little black boy and say "Yes sir, no sir" all the damned time.'

Sunny's mind was elsewhere. 'Leave all that, bru, just now that Johnny fuller is going to come here.'

'Which Johnny?' The Stranger was somewhat taken aback.

– *That fuller interfering with the old man's daughter.*

– *You sure it's him, Sunny?*

– *Must be him. He comes here every afternoon to pull fahfee. If anybody interfering with girl in Mount Edgecombe, it must be that Johnny fuller.*

– *Then why didn't you tell the old man?*

– *No, bru, the old man will only mess things up. I got one plan, see.*

– *Yeah, you're right we've got to handle this very carefully. But I've got to deliver a parcel around here first. I've got to see Mr MP Naidoo, the school principal. School must have finished by now. You know where he lives?*

– *Oh that principal fuller. Short bald-headed fuller? Right! You go down the Main Road. Next turn right. Then you take 'nother one turn left, Rawalpindi Road – third house, with a maroon roof.*

The Stranger finished his drink. 'Thanks, I'll be back as soon as I deliver the parcel. Now, if this Johnny chap gets here before I get back, try to keep him here. Just get him talking. When I get back we'll put the screws on him. We've just got to help the old man out. I'll be back as soon as I can.'

Chapter Four

The Stranger hurried through his delivery and made it back just before Johnny arrived. Johnny came to the bar a few times a day touting for fahfee customers. Fahfee was a numbers game. An investment of a few bob could net you a decent return. It was a question of having the right dream. The 'Chinaman' who headed the ring ensured that printed lists of numbers associated with objects from pigs to popcorn were well circulated. You dreamt of a certain object, you hit that number. When the number was 'pulled' it was not a coincidence – it was most certainly a gesture from the heavens. The 'Chinaman' together with Johnny, was a firm believer that a sucker was born everyday, which explains why he was able to drive from pub to pub in a late model Mercedes Benz. Johnny didn't do too badly either, although this was essentially a front for far more profitable rackets.

The Stranger was relieved to hear that Johnny had not arrived yet. He and Sunny would pretend they knew nothing of the incident with Mothie's daughter. They went over the plan again. As Sunny put it, 'That's right. We'll act like we don't know nothing. Then we'll slowly fish him out.'

'Right,' said the Stranger. 'We must find out where the girl is first ...'

There was a sudden loud sound of music, and Sunny

whispered, 'Ssssh, here he comes now.'

Johnny, suave in the coolest gear and longish hair and carrying a large ghettoblaster, danced his way in.

Sunny spoke loudly over the music to the Stranger. 'Lot of China-guava trees in Cato Manor, eh?'

The Stranger nodded in agreement as Johnny put his tape player on the table and did a few nifty dance steps to the music. He hailed the two men – 'Hi Sunny! Hi there!'

Sunny was all smiles as he said, 'Hello Johnny. Put that damn thing slowly, man.'

– *Whatsa matter, you don't appreciate good music?*

– *You call that good music?*

– *Give me a pint of ice-cold beer, dad.*

– *You can't even hear what the singer is singing. Good music!*

– *That's the style, dad, you gotta get with it.*

– *Turn that thing slow, Johnny, man. What my lahnee will say, man…*

Johnny reluctantly obliged, and turned down the volume.

– *What's doh-die today?*

– *Thirty-six.*

– *Last night I dreamt of lot of frogs. What number is frogs?*

– *Frogs? That should be the same as fish – that's number 24.*

– *Okay, play me sixty cents on number 24.*

Not a gambling man, the Stranger skipped the game but someone had to get Johnny chatting. Did he make enough cash through all this activity of his? Johnny was the soul of modesty. 'It's okay.'

Sunny chipped in. 'Don't worry about this fuller, bru.

He's a fantastic soccer player. Hey, Johnny, that goal you scored … What a goal! That choothia ref said offside. His uncle, offside!'

Johnny continued to be the soul of modesty. 'You know how it goes, bru, you win some, you lose some.'

Sunny kept going as Johnny's praise singer. 'He's also a small-time lahnee, bru. You want to buy tape recorder, those dirty books they keep underneath? See Johnny.'

'Anything pal, anything.' The laaitie was into his stride. 'You name it, Johnny's got it.'

Sunny winked at the Stranger. 'Plenty of dames too, eh?'

'Span, eksê!'

Sunny winked again at the Stranger. 'I hear you got a crazy bok in Mount Edgecombe?'

– *All over, dad, all over. I pitch my tent in one spot and if I like it, I stick around for a while. Then I split. I'm like lightning – I never strike twice in the same spot.*

– *Okay, Lightning, who is this crazy bok in Mount Edgecombe?*

– *She's lekker, eksê, crazy pair of legs, long black hair and crazy tits. Hey, who told you about this bok?*

– *Everybody knows Johnny around here.*

– *But nobody saw me with her. She's a home bird, you know what I mean. Nice clean dame. It's a crazy set-up – there's no one at home during the day. She's alone.*

The Stranger was right on cue. 'Pardon me for asking, but is she in love with you?'

Johnny grinned. 'Love is for the birds.'

The Stranger was not to be put off. 'That's how you feel. What about her?'

Johnny kept grinning, took another sip and said, 'Yeah, she's in love with me. She wants to marry me.'

The Stranger asked, 'So why don't you marry her?'

The grin was still there. 'You know any more jokes?'

'How can you do that to a nice girl like that?' Sunny demanded.

The grin was wearing thin. 'She is a nice girl. She's never had a boyfriend before. She'll make some lucky guy a very nice wife …'

The Stranger persevered asking who would marry her after Johnny had been messing around with her. For Johnny this wasn't his affair – hell, he hadn't raped her. The Stranger insisted that was not the point.

'It's none of your damn business,' Johnny fired back, 'but okay, hold on, you're so crazy to know, I'll tell you how I met her. I was driving down the road when I saw this chick. I slowed down and I hooted. She didn't even look at me. I said, "Howzit Baby!" Made like she didn't hear me. I turned my car around and I stopped. She was going to the shop. When she came out she didn't even look at me. I reckon, I'm going to get you, baby. I waited for her at the same spot for three days and then she stopped one day and said, "Haven't you got any work to do?" "I reckon I'm my own boss." Then I asked her how she liked my tape 'Khabi Khabi' – I was sommer vasing it loud …'

'She must have been deaf like you.' Sunny couldn't resist the crack.

Johnny ignored him. 'She smiled – but just then someone walked past and she walked away. I followed her and we started talking about music, and then just like that – now she's in love with me.'

A thought crossed the Stranger's mind. If he had been in Johnny's shoes, he'd definitely have jerked it off instead of spoiling a good girl. Out loud he said it somewhat differently:

Johnny must have told her he loved her a lot and probably offered to marry her, otherwise she wouldn't have gone to bed with him – 'Isn't that right?'

The grin disappeared completely. Johnny got up. 'Who said she went to bed with me?'

– Come on Johnny, I know you're a shark.

– I told her no such thing – I told her I smaak her a span, no promises, nothing.

– That's the same as telling her you're in love with her.

The Stranger agreed loudly. Johnny's suspicions were aroused. 'Hey, hold on. What are you guys getting at?'

– What you mean what we're getting at?

– The way you guys are asking me questions it looks as if you guys have got something up your sleeves.

The Stranger tried to assure him: they didn't even know the girl. Sunny added with emphasis, 'But I got a daughter and I don't like anyone treating her like that. Look, bru, if I catch any of these fullers treating her like that I will kill them, me. I'll kill them!'

Johnny shook his head. 'Your daughter may love the guy.'

– Bullshit, love only comes after you get married and have children. She wants to go out with someone, he must bring his mother and father by her home first. Hell, in our days if we wanted to take a girl out we had to marry her even if we took our mother and father by the girl's house.

– That's your days, dad, not today.

'Girls are too free these days,' the Stranger put in, 'which is why they get into trouble so much.'

Johnny's grin was as annoying as his assessment, 'You guys must have had a hard time. What did you do for fun – play marbles?'

147

The Stranger retorted, 'What do you think your mother and father did before they got married?'

Even if Johnny thought his Fadda was an arsehole, nobody had the right to impugn his parents. He struggled to keep his cool. He'd have grabbed the bottle if these guys had been younger. Instead he said somewhat menacingly, 'There's no need to pick on my parents.'

The Stranger realised he had gone too far. 'No need to get upset, Johnny. We're just having a friendly discussion.'

For Johnny this was really pushing it. Picking up his tape player, he warned them – 'Watch it, you're getting too personal' –and stormed out, this time without music.

The Stranger was contrite. 'Looks like we blew it.'

'Don't worry,' Sunny said, 'He'll be back just now when all the workers come here. He'll be back before then. Good thing he left too, because Mothie could be back any time.'

The Stranger smiled. 'That's good, we can still trap him. We can't allow him to abuse a girl from a good family and get away with it. But Mothie must know where the girl is, that's the main thing. We must help the old man find his daughter. Another drink, please.'

Sunny was about to expand on his ideas to trap Johnny when Mothie returned. He was very angry. 'Who's that fuller left here just now? He got no bloody respect, that bloody swine. He going so fast he nearly knock me.'

– *What, with his car?*

– *No, with his body. He didn't say sorry, nothing. He jumped in his bloody car and vroom, vroom, he skidded the car. What he thinks, he's a racing driver?*

– *Leave all that. What happened when you went police station?*

– *Hey, they was very nice, man. Hey, call Mr So-So, I*

want to thank him – they was very nice, man.

– What happened?

– I went there. That same police fuller was there. I said I want to see Sergeant Lab – what the name the boss gave?

'Labooshain.' The Stranger helpfully pronounced it the French way. Sunny corrected him: 'Hey, what Labooshain? This is a boere fuller. His name is Labuskaknee! Kaknee!'

– Same one, same one. I said I want to see him. Hell, that Indian fuller got frightened. He say, 'Don't worry you can give me your complaint.' He spoke so nice to me. Sergeant Labuskakne came out and he say, 'Musi, Moosa, take a van and go and find that girl now.' Moosa's face went away like a samoosa! I took him home and I showed him a photo of my daughter. He's looking for her now. In the van he's talking so nicely to me. He don't know all the lahnee in Mount Edgecombe my friends. He don't know me yet.

Was this a recent photo, the Stranger wanted to know. 'Ya,' said Mothie. 'They took in the wedding. My cousin daughter got married. They took in the wedding. Gimme some more wine. Yeah, now they looking for her. That Moosa fuller don't know me yet.'

The Stranger laughed. 'I'll bet he knows you now!'

Mothie had proved his point. Now he wanted to thank the lahnee. Sunny gave him his wine. Mothie had brought more money from home and he offered a dop to the Stranger, who politely refused. Mothie kept insisting until Sunny stopped him, 'What you keep asking like a tape recorder? Take your drink and sit down there.'

They led him to a table and the Stranger assured him that his daughter would be found now that they had a picture of her. Mothie moaned, 'I don't know where she is. I don't know what she done with herself …'

– *Don't talk like that, Mothie. She must be with one of her friends. Just because you hit her one time, you mustn't worry. You did the right thing. She'll learn her lesson. She must know she comes from a good family. Don't worry. God is watching.*

– *Ram, Ram, I'm praying she don't do something funny with herself. But she haven't got sari.*

– *What do you mean by that?*

– *She haven't got sari. You don't know what sari is, you?*

– *I know what sari is, but why you say she haven't got sari?*

– *You don't read newspapers, what?*

– *What the hell do you mean, Mothie, talking gibberish!*

– *You don't read in the newspapers everyday girls taking sari from the wardrobe and hanging themselves from the mango tree …*

Sunny threw up his hands in despair. The Stranger, again struck by life's absurdities, tried to calm the old man's fears. 'Don't jump to conclusions, Uncle. Mount Edgecombe is a small place. The police will find your daughter soon. Have your wine.'

Mothie took his advice, drained the glass and ordered another, which Sunny willingly supplied, this time on the house. It didn't come from his pocket, of course. He would remember to make up for it during the stock-take. His arithmetic never failed him even in moments of crisis. Mothie didn't take much time in draining that too.

– *Wine is the best thing, eh, bhai? Every day you work, you work, work, work – that's all. You don't look for trouble. Why God must do this to me?*

– *That's your karma, Mothie. Can't get away from that.*

– *Every time I go temple. I do puja, I do everything. Why*

*God must do this to me? Wine is the best thing – gimme '
nother one wine.*

Sunny felt that the old man had had enough. 'Take it easy.
Wine is okay but it won't solve your problems.

He was up against a tough old customer. 'If I want to
drink wine, my business. You think I'm drunk what? See
here I can stand on one leg …'

He tried it and stumbled. The Stranger, showing remarkable
reflexes although he himself had had more than his usual
limit, was about to grab him. Mothie steadied himself as best
he could and pushed him away. 'You leave me alone. Sunny
says I'm drunk. I'll prove to him I'm not drunk.' The old
man lifted up one leg and tottered. He was about to hit the
floor when the Stranger, now closer and fully in anticipation,
grabbed him. A silly grin of embarrassment broke on
Mothie's face. 'Hell, I'm tired, man.'

This was more than enough for both Sunny and the
Stranger. The Stranger for the first time raised his voice: 'You
better stop this nonsense!'

They half-carried Mothie to the chair at the table and
dumped him on it. Mothie was still adamant he was not
drunk. He tried to stand again, saying as he swayed, 'Hell,
I'm just tired, all I need is 'nother one wine and you see how
straight I'll stand.'

With that, his brief attempt at being vertical failed and he
flopped on the chair. It was too much for Sunny. 'Just shut
up and sit there. We're trying our best to help you and you
carrying on like this!'

The Stranger agreed. 'Yes, we can find your daughter if
you behave yourself.' Through the alcoholic mists clouding
Mothie's mind, a bit of clarity emerged. 'You know where
my daughter is?' All the Stranger could say was they felt that

they could help to find her.

By now the lahnee had come into the bar, hearing Mothie's tantrums. He was annoyed, which was nothing unusual, especially after the Tennysonian episode. He barked, 'Oh no, not you again!'

All Mothie could see was his benefactor. 'Oh hello, boss, thank you, boss. The police was so nice to me. Thank you, boss!'

This display of servility found its mark. So-So preened himself and grabbed the opportunity to play the expected role of the lahnee to the hilt. His laugh had the right patronising touch. Adding a crude Indian accent he said, 'Don't worry, Uncle, don't worry. The polices will find your daughter. Just sit down same place and catch one dop.'

Mothie complained, 'But Sunny don't want to give me wine.'

The lahnee was actually playful as he teased Sunny. 'Silly fuller you, I give you one shot just now! Give him one dop. Otherwise I fix you up!'

Power was a sure-fire tonic for self-restoration. As he strode out, feeling a bigger man than he had for some time, he uttered, with even more pointed consonants and even more rounded vowels, 'Bloody idiots!'

Mothie had nothing but admiration for his considerate lahnee. 'Lekker lahnee, see how he likes me!'

The Stranger thumped his fist on the table almost upsetting his glass of cane. 'You see, how they talk to us, Sunny!'

Jolted by the sudden show of emotion, Sunny tried to placate him. 'Don't worry, man.'

– *They think we're a bunch of idiots.*

– *Let them think what they want as long as we know we're not idiots.*

Sunny's brand of self-belief didn't wash with the Stranger. 'I just don't like their bloody attitude.'

Sunny, the eternal pacifist, was philosophical. 'That's life. You got the clever fullers one side and you got the stupid fullers one side. Clever fullers don't want to act clever. If you want to get somewhere you must act stupid.'

The Stranger wasn't listening. Philistinism, in all its thuggishness, had forced its way to centre stage. The image of the jailbird in a loincloth making a pair of shoes for his jailer, which he had promised himself he would summon at such times, had completely vanished from his mind. In short, at that moment, he saw things in stark black and white, not in technicolour. 'Just who the hell do they think they are? What makes them so damn superior? You know something, when these guys were walking around in caves wearing animal skins, our people were building temples in India. When they were hanging on to raw meat, our people were cooking their food … and you know something else? Counting, numerals. They learnt it from us, they learnt it from the Indians. Now they walk all over us and you guys just sit there – yes sir, no sir. God you make me sick!'

Sunny refused to take this personally. He said with even greater sang-froid, 'Talking about Indian fullers, I'm remembering something. You know when that great Indian singer Pithikuli Murugadas came to this country, he said, you all laughing because I'm speaking English like this. Imagine how I'm laughing when you all speaking Tamil!'

– *I just can't understand you chaps, Sunny!*

– *Look, bru, I may act stupid but I know what I'm doing. Look, I'm a barman, but I got my own house, I got my own car. Nothing short in my house. I give my family everything. Nothing short in my house.*

153

Mothie, who had been trying to make sense of what was being said, laughed until he nearly fell off the chair. 'Barmans clever fullers, bhai. When nobody looking they pour short tots.'

– *When you saw me pouring short tots, eh, when you saw me pouring short tots?*

– *I never saw you. You too clever you. You got the draat. Nev'mine, that's your business.*

– *I don't do things like that. I don't pour short tots. I work hard, me.*

No way could the Stranger continue Sunny's political education under these conditions. There was a different kind of logic here. Sunny was not being paid his due. So what if he dipped his hand in the cookie jar? After all, he had helped fill it up. 'I'm sure you do,' he told him kindly.

Sunny was still indignant. 'I don't do things like that. I don't want to be like that Johnny fuller. I don't want to go to jail. I don't want to be like that Johnny fuller.'

Too late. The Stranger frowned at this lapse. The cat was out of the bag. Mothie demanded, 'Which Johnny?'

The Stranger was a man of integrity. There was no point avoiding the issue any longer. He looked straight at Sunny. 'You'd better tell him.'

Sunny took a deep breath and said, 'Same ou.'

'What you mean same ou?' Mothie was sitting very still now.

– *Same ou messing around with your daughter.*

– *You know him?*

– *He was here just now.*

– *Where's he? Where's that bloody bastard? I'll kill him.*

– *Same fuller knocked you before.*

– *That fuller with the long hair?*

– Same ou.

– Then why you never tell me?

*– **We got one plan …***

The Stranger added that Johnny was coming back soon. Sunny urged Mothie, 'First you must listen to us – we'll trap him.'

– I don't want to trap him, I want to kill him!

– Don't be silly, Mothie. We're trying to help you. Just shut up and listen.

Temporarily common sense seemed to prevail and Mothie said, 'Awright.'

– He's going to come back just now. I know him, he comes here to pull fahfee.

– That's the fuller, huh? I saw him here once or twice. I don't play fahfee. I don't gamble. Gambling very bad – devil's job. How you know same fuller?

– He told us.

– What he told you?

– You wasting time. He's going to come back just now. Now you must listen to us.

The Stranger stretched out and held Mothie's elbow. 'Uncle, you must listen to Sunny. We must find your daughter. When Johnny comes back you must act like you don't know him.'

'Act like I don't know him! I'll take this bottle and break it on his head! Act like I don't know him …'

The Stranger was losing patience. 'You just go and do that, and if your daughter hasn't committed suicide already then she'll definitely commit suicide if you kill Johnny.'

'Then I won't kill him,' Mothie replied, 'I'll cripple him!'

'Shut up and listen.' Sunny stood over him. 'You must act like you don't know him. We'll talk to him. Then we'll ask him who this girl is, what he did to her, you mustn't say one word.'

The Stranger took it further. 'We'll be your witnesses. What's your daughter's age?'

'Fifteen.' They were aghast. 'Fifteen! You can charge him because she's under age.' 'But', Sunny added, 'we won't charge him if he tells us where your daughter is and if he agrees to marry her.'

Mothie was adamant. 'I don't want my daughter to marry rubbish fuller like that. What work he does?'

Sunny said he didn't have a regular job, and the Stranger said, 'That's right, he only pulls fahfee. But he's an intelligent chap and he could get a good job.' Sunny said that Johnny had more money than Sunny and Mothie put together. He knew Johnny well. He was a bright chap with a bright future.

Mothie remained unimpressed.

'But he's a rubbish fuller …'

Even in half-expectancy, the loud sound of a tape player shook them with nerve-jangling suddenness.

Chapter Five

They drove and drove. They trudged and trudged. They knocked and knocked. The girl was nowhere to be found and what's more the Heat was Very Hot. Moosa was of the view that they should take a break. Musi agreed. Moosa suggested, 'Let's get a bunny-chow there by Goolam's Take-Away.'

Musi was not too fond of bunny-chow. In the wrong hands it could hide many sins such as a preponderance of gristle, skin and fat and very little, if any, real meat. It was the same with mass-produced meat pies. Musi abhorred them too. He was talking from experience. His ample potbelly bore witness. He also knew all the eateries in and around Mount Edgecombe. Goolam's was not where you could buy a really good bunny-chow, even if you were a cop. He'd rather have tandoori chicken, as hot as you please. With tandoori chicken you got what you saw.

They parked their van under the shade of a flamboyant laden with sprays of fresh blooms. Moosa tucked into the bunny-chow with gusto. Looking at the picture of Mothie's daughter on the dashboard, he winked at Musi and in between mouthfuls said, 'Lekker chick, eksê. Don't mind checking her out myself.'

Musi clicked his tongue in disapproval. 'Hau, she's like your daughter, you old bull!'

When they finished, they continued driving around the district. It was high noon and they still hadn't found the girl. It wouldn't do to go back to Labuschagne empty-handed after he had demanded that they find the girl.

Then a brilliant idea struck Musi. 'I know who can help us!' When he heard who, Moosa said, 'We got to be careful. If this gets out we could get into trouble with old Kaknee, let alone becoming laughing stocks in the district.' Musi agreed, 'Ya, that Kaknee is full of kak.'

They drove to Bulala Tshabalala's kraal on the outskirts of the district. It was perched on a hill. Huge sisal and thorn-laden aloe plants and monstrous, impenetrable cacti and thorn bush surrounded a rondavel-like brick structure with a thatched roof. Outside the house stood two cars: a gleaming late-model Mercedes Benz and an old beat-up Volkswagen station wagon that was used to negotiate potholed roads for house visits. There were two huge gargoyle-like statues, half crocodile and half man, flanking the door. Tshabalala, adorned with a hyena skin, a crown of crocodile teeth around the crown of his head, fly-whisk in his hand, goat skins around his wrist, and not much else, welcomed them with a huge smile. It was always good to have the cops on your side. There was a long queue of people that stretched far down the hill. The cops jumped the queue. This consultation was for free and they sat on lion skins on the floor as he threw his bones.

As he did so he went into a trance. His eyes rolled and his voice changed. 'I see a bad spirit sitting on her. We must chase the bad spirit from her otherwise you will never get her back.'

Musi ventured meekly, 'Where is she?'

Tshabalala threw the bones again, did a weird dance

around them, knelt down, staring closely at them. 'Patience, patience, it says here she will be found, but we must chase the powerful spirit that is making her do this. Don't worry, I will send my tikoloshe to chase the spirit away. Tell her father to see me. Because of you I shall charge him a special good price.'

As they walked down the hill in silent thought they felt relieved that the medicine man had said that she would be found. That was good enough. They weren't told to chase away any spirit that was haunting her. All they had to do was to find her. They continued searching for Mothie's daughter.

Back at the White House Hotel, with his tape player blaring, Johnny danced his way into the bar just as the Stranger and Sunny succeeded temporarily in quietening Mothie down.

Sunny quickly changed the subject, 'Nice place, London eh, bru?' The Stranger nodded strenuously and greeted Johnny. 'Hi Johnny, good to see you back. I'm sorry I upset you. I didn't mean to offend you. Good to see you back.'

Johnny nodded acceptance of the apology as he changed the cassette, 'You still here? It's no big deal. How's this number?'

Sunny tried to heighten the newfound camaraderie. 'He was only chuning, bru. Come on, have a beer on me. Lekker number but put it slowly, eksê. You know the lahnee's next door.'

Switching off his player, Johnny advised Sunny to tell his lahnee to go back where he came from, 'from where they didn't know how to joll, eksê. And don't worry about the beer. You know I don't have more than one before graf.'

The Stranger took the beer from Sunny and handed it to Johnny. 'Aw, come on, one two beers are not going to make you drunk.'

Johnny sipped the beer and the Stranger told him there was a vacancy at his firm for a clerk. He had plenty of say and he could fix him up. Johnny warmed to the growing chumminess, but couldn't resist a bit of cheek: 'Suddenly you guys smaak me. When must I have my hair cut?'

The Stranger said he was very serious about 'our young chaps making it in life – especially intelligent chaps like you.' Johnny asked what the pay was. A hundred and twenty a month, the Stranger replied. Johnny blinked. 'You gotta be joking. That's peanuts.'

Sunny felt the young hustler was being too smart. 'What you mean, peanuts? I only get a hundred a month.'

Johnny pounced, 'That's okay for monkeys like you.'

– Hey you watch your tongue, you. I work honest job. I'm not ashamed of myself.

– Okay, okay, don't get so worked up. I also worked honest once. I left school because my parents couldn't afford to send me like. I worked in this spares shop in Pinetown. Then this honkey joined us. He was a foreigner and couldn't even speak English properly. I had to teach this ou everything, even to speak proper English. Then they promoted him above me, and what's worse he started pushing me around. How do you like that?

For the Stranger that's what it was all about and he fully sympathised. Same bloody scene all over!

Johnny went on. 'I took a good look around. Char ous were working there for years, longer than some of the honkeys, but they weren't getting more than what the laaitie honkeys were getting, even the foreigners!'

The Stranger's hackles rose even more. 'And they just sit back and take everything.'

Johnny was obviously different. 'Not me, eksê! One day I told this honkey, up yours! I quit right then and there. I tried to find another job.'

Sunny was as practical as ever. 'If you don't like working for wit ous, why don't you work for char ous?'

Johnny's immediate response was, Char Ous are worse than the honkeys – they make you graf in your lunchtime and all. 'Yeah, I tell you, I looked all over for a job, looking in the newspapers, going for interviews, but everywhere I went they offered me peanuts and the char ous – they offered me stale peanuts. Then I thought why don't you be your own boss. That was it. I want to tell you something – I make more money in one month than you guys make in three months.'

Strongly as he disapproved of breaking the law, the Stranger conceded that in another way Johnny's actions were understandable, but Sunny was very clear about the consequences of such action. 'The cops are going to get you one day.'

'Don't tell me about cops,' Johnny said. 'They're bigger crooks than I'll ever be.'

The Stranger wanted to know what Johnny was going to do with his money, and Johnny didn't mind telling him. 'I'm going to pull out of this country, man. There's no future here. Out there there's a whole lot of living. I want to go to a place where I can get the chance to live like a human being. Here you walk into a bazaar and some cheap honkey tit treats you like dirt.'

Running away wouldn't solve problems was wise advice but not what Johnny needed to hear. 'Who wants to solve problems? I got no time, daddyo, I just want to live, man, live.'

Mothie had kept his feelings to himself for far too long.

He fairly exploded, 'You not worried about your mother and your father, you?!'

Johnny said they could take care of themselves. Before they could stop him, Mothie was up from his chair shouting, 'Hey, you got no respect, you? If it wasn't for your mother and your father you wouldn't be here.'

Sunny shot out from behind the counter. With the help of the Stranger they managed to get Mothie back to his chair. Johnny looked puzzled and the Stranger tried to divert attention. Not everything was rosy overseas, he argued. The cost of living was much higher there. 'I was telling Sunny I was overseas recently. I agree with you. It's a whole new world. You can feel the freedom out there – and if a black guy can work half as hard as he works here he can earn himself a comfortable living.'

For Johnny the higher cost of living was no big deal. 'That's nothing, what about the women?'

The Stranger turned away in mild disgust. 'Is that all you think about?'

Sunny was far more disgusted. 'Nothing else in your bloody head but only girls!'

Perched on his bar stool, Johnny took a swig, swung one leg over the other and said with a grin, 'Too much, daddyo, too much!'

This was too much for Mothie. He was on his feet again yelling, 'Hey, where you come from, where you come from?'

Johnny, still on his stool, replied, 'Timbucktoo, where do you come from?'

This was the last straw for Mothie. 'Timbucktoo! Timbucktoo! You got no respect! I'll show you ...'

Mothie stumbled towards him. Grabbing him, the Stranger

was apologetic. 'He's upset over something …'

Mothie continued yelling. 'I'm not upset! What you saying I'm upset. I just want to give him one shot. I'll give you hiding like your father never gave you!'

Johnny was up from his stool. 'Old man like you?!'

Mothie, wrenching free, grabbed a bottle from the table. 'Old man? You calling me old man?'

While Sunny held Mothie down, the Stranger came in between him and Johnny and said firmly above the din, 'Sit down, both of you.'

Sunny was shouting at Mothie, 'Just leave it to us, we will help you.'

It occurred to Johnny that something was going on, something he was not privy to. 'What the hell is going on here?'

The Stranger spelt it out. 'You're in big trouble.'

Johnny was incredulous, 'Who, me?'

Sunny demanded, 'Where did you take the girl to?'

Johnny was even more incredulous, 'What girl?'

The Stranger was no longer open to being impartial. 'The girl you were telling us about. Come on, don't pretend like you didn't do anything. If you tell us where the girl is we'll sort this out without going to the police.'

For Johnny this was going much too far. He picked up his tape player. 'You guys must be crazy. I don't know what you're talking about. If you feel like playing games, go find yourself another playmate. I'm getting sick and tired of this crap.'

He headed for the door. The Stranger blocked his way. 'What's the hurry?'

Emboldened by the Stranger's move, Mothie grabbed a bottle but swiftly put it down the moment Johnny whipped out a knife. Desperately trying to get out of range, Mothie cowered behind the table screaming blue murder – 'Watch out, that fuller got a knife!'

The Stranger circled his man. It was clear that he was streetwise despite his posh cufflinks. Johnny lunged at him three times; each time the Stranger sidestepped with the aplomb of a matador. On the fourth lunge the Stranger grabbed his wrist and overpowered him with Mothie yelling a mixture of obscenities and appeals to the Gods. The huge din attracted the attention of the lahnee who appeared behind the counter demanding, 'What the hell is going on here?'

Everyone froze. Mothie shouted, 'That's the fuller, boss, that's the fuller!'

Johnny yelled back, 'Old man, get off my bloody back!'

The lahnee was in a mean mood. 'Shut up, both of you. Will somebody tell me what exactly is going on?'

Mothie, re-energised by the presence of the lahnee, grabbed the bottle. Johnny put up his fists in defence with Mothie doing a weird to and fro at him. The lahnee shouted again, 'If both of you don't sit down, I'll throw you out. Carrying on like a bunch of idiots.'

Just then, the phone rang. Still glaring at them, he picked up the receiver. 'Hello. Yes. Oh hello, Sergeant. Yes, he's right here, carrying on like a bloody idiot. What? No, that *can't* be, they've got the culprit right here. Are you sure? Well that sorts out everything. Where? I'll tell Mothie that. Thanks a lot. Drop in for a pint sometime. Bye.'

The word Sergeant told Mothie that was the police talking. 'Good job! The police coming to take that fuller away.'

Johnny got up to leave again but the Stranger apologetically held him back. Johnny moved to the stool and hissed, 'Shit!'

What the lahnee had to say next shook everyone. 'You got

the wrong man, Mothie.'

Mothie swallowed hard and spoke into the short, astonished silence.

'Don't joke, boss, this no time for jokes.'

The lahnee insisted. 'I said you got the wrong man.' Yes, the phone call was from Sergeant Labuschagne. They had found Mothie's daughter after a neighbour had alerted them. The image of the man in a loincloth dropped off the Stranger's radar screen completely as the chuckling lahnee announced, in what he obviously felt were pukka Indian accents, 'They found her by one fuller's house. That fuller say he going to marry your daughter. Now you going to have one big, big wedding. Don't forget to bring me some curry and rice.'

Mothie felt he had stepped out of jail into the sunshine and blue skies. The lahnee called for a round of drinks. 'Hey, Mothie, have one 'nother one wine – and give these chaps a drink too.'

The Stranger shook his head and turned to go. 'No thanks, I'm leaving.'

The lahnee was in an expansive mood. 'Aw, come on, Sammy, have one on me.'

Whipping round, he said in steady tones which heightened the hostility, 'My name is not Sammy. You have no right to call me Sammy.'

Sunny and Mothie were aghast. No one had ever spoken to the lahnee like that. Mothie tried desperately to revive the fast-fading camaraderie. Holding the Stranger by the hand he said, 'Boss only joking, bhai ...'

The Stranger kept staring at the lahnee. His tone was still measured. 'Leave me alone.'

Mothie persisted, trying to coax him back towards the bar. This time the tone was harsh and final as he angrily shoved the old man aside, 'I said leave me alone, you fool!'

Shocked into silence, the lahnee could only stand and stare. The Stranger made for the door, kicked over a chair on his way, stopped and whirled on the lahnee. His tone was not measured any more, it was unrestrained, all malevolence and foreboding. 'One day, white man! One day!' And he disappeared into the darkness.

The lahnee was aware that everyone was looking at him, but this time the consonants were not so pointed and his vowels not so rounded. 'He's just done himself out of a drink. You get these damn agitators everywhere!'

Mothie comforted him. 'Don't worry about him, boss. You want I must sing for you, boss?'

'Yes, come on, Mothie.' Why not?

Mothie stood up unexpectedly straight. 'I can dance for you too, boss.'

Johnny sat sullenly on his stool. Mothie's singing hit the highest decibel count he could manage. Offkey, offbeat, what the hell! The break was welcome for the lahnee, who joined in the clapping as Sunny hammered out a canny beat on the counter and Mothie danced the Natchannia with gusto.

Epilogue

Is there such a thing as a real final curtain? Life just seems to go on and on, no matter what went before, unless there's a nuclear Armageddon that's like the Big Bang. It must be conceded that such an event, according to one George Bush and one Mahmoud Ahmadinejad, is not entirely beyond the bounds of possibility, in which case there could be a final curtain. There are those who say that even then, in an infinite universe, life would be lurking in some form, possibly even resembling that endangered specimen, Mr So-So.

Koodikaran, like the Stranger, was also moved to ponder the great mystery of life and death after a particularly heavy binge. Prior to that, someone asked Koodikaran, in one of his more lucid moments, whether he was not afraid of death (given the dangers he exposed himself to by constantly drinking himself into a stupor). Koodikaran's response had a philosophic bent that seemed admirable, given the fact that he could barely lift his head off the table at the time. 'Billions have died before me, millions are dying right now and billions will die after me. So what is so special about you and me that we should be the exceptions?'

Koodikaran was to learn that death scares the shit out of even the most rational mind. Koodikaran, like Chaka Ronnie, could also not eat on an empty liver. Unlike Chaka Ronnie, there were days when he hardly ate anything. Came the day when he had not eaten a morsel and he had had put away enough leftover alcohol to fell an ox. Throughout the day he gulped down beer, cane spirits, vodka, brandy, Scotch, gin, what ever came his way as leftovers in the glasses of patrons who'd had enough – a really potent mix. He was just able to stagger out the door when he collapsed in a heap. He was so dehydrated that his sugar had dropped to the dangerous level of two. Fortunately they could rush him to hospital and give him an intravenous drip in time. When he recovered consciousness the doctor told him he'd been extremely fortunate. Not only could he have suffered brain damage, he was indeed seconds away from being ushered into the Great Beyond. That was enough to sober him up for the rest of his life. Philosophy and rationale went out the window. Despite the billions dying before and after him, he got the fright of his life. The realisation sank home that his time in the world was indeed special.

That idea also occurred to several other players in this lascivious legend after their own cathartic experiences, resulting in changes in their lives either for good or bad.

The Stranger never got to figure out what the ding-dong life was all about but he finally figured out that the better way to tackle philistinism was to tackle it at its root. That would take some time and indeed it was a Long Walk. In the end it didn't matter whether it was a Wit Ou, a Char Ou, a Bruin Ou or a Pekkie Ou – a Philistine was a Philistine. It was fine to get even on a personal level, as he had done when he confronted the Lahnee, but only up to a point; and it was futile if you didn't understand this elementary piece of common sense, that there's a limit.

It was also futile if you thought you could tackle the issue on your own. He joined the Natal Indian Congress and threw himself into its activities both above and under ground. In time he received a visit from the Special Branch and was told, 'Watch it, jong!' That didn't deter him and he was soon nominated for the post of assistant secretary. It seemed a cakewalk but his former student comrade beat him to it. Shaik had the ruling elite of the Congress, somewhat unkindly referred to as the Cabal, in his back pocket. The Stranger was too much of a straight shooter to take Shaik on at his own game. It was so frustrating, he almost started jerking again. Anyway, perhaps it was a stroke of luck that he was prevented from taking on an extra load of work – he was now able to put in more effort towards his dream of owning his own stationers'. A few years later he opened a shop, Rainbow Stationers, on the walls of which he proudly put up posters of Che Guevara and Nelson Mandela.

Thankfully for The Stranger, Hawa Bib Majumdar hadn't got over him. Neither had he got over her. He bumped into her one day on a busy Saturday morning in Victoria Street, Durban. Their reunion was quite dramatic. Like the first time, they didn't say a word to each other. The old fire was still there. There were a couple of heavily bearded shopkeepers standing at the entrances to their shops touting for business, but this did not deter either of them. They were soon locked in tight embrace as if this time they weren't going to let go. The beards wagged furiously but holding hands they went into Pyramid Jewéllers and The Stranger bought a wedding ring then and there.

Our Lady of Shalott, who in South Africa hadn't had the slightest interest in politics, founded the Hampstead Anti-apartheid Society. More importantly she finished writing her play, *Alas, Poor Fanyana*. When we last heard of her she was still trying to find someone to play the role of Fanyana.

Unfortunately, there was no one who could fit into his size of jockstrap, which had been specially made for him, and the dimensions of which she was so well acquainted with. As for Fanyana, he was forced to abandon his studies and left the country to join Umkhonto we Sizwe, where he rapidly rose to the position of Field Colonel. As committed as he was to the Struggle, he was still very much a lady's man. Although he never used a condom he made sure he protected himself. He took care to have a shower after every dingging encounter.

Johnny, despite his long-held aversion to marriage, made the mistake of striking twice in the same spot. The second time round, in the heat of passion, he realised he didn't have a condom at hand. With 'Khabi Khabi' playing at full volume on his ghettoblaster to mask the searing sounds of passion, nature took its course. It was the most creative goal he had scored in his life, as a result of which, Poolmathie had taken the first step to motherhood. Although it was a shotgun wedding it was a grand one. Kamatchi and Koonthie helped prepare the food to cater for the whole of Mount Edgecombe. Every Char Ou turned up, as well as some Bruin Ous and Pekkie Ous too. Indeed, there was a noticeable absence of Wit Ous. Blithering Idiot No 1 and Mothie, now a grandfather of a bouncing baby girl, were also there, 'suit, boot and all'.

The Stranger was guest speaker at the wedding and couldn't resist beginning his speech by saying that Johnny had once likened himself to lightning but failed to stick to the rule that lightening never strikes twice in the same spot. It seems that his bride was so alluring that he couldn't help breaking this time-honoured practice. Everyone roared with laughter, including Johnny. We apologise for not mentioning earlier that Johnny's surname was Veerappen and he was a Mandraji Ou. His radiant bride, Poolmathie Pookun, was a

Roti. Thus two bands were in attendance – Suhana Sanjith, whose hit number was 'Hey Ganga Maiya', and Luxmi Entertainers, with their 'Bomme Bomme'. At the height of the nuptials, though, both combined to play 'Khabi Khabi'.

As for Black Cat Bambata, he had forgotten his grudge against Fanyana but not about how Moosa's Outfitters had ripped him off. He realised he could not only get even with Char Ous but also make far more money by joining Inkatha and becoming one of the headman's collectors. Inkatha's unofficial slogan was, 'Ubuntu only for the Bantu!' He had spent time with Sunny, learning how to fiddle the funds. In time he was promoted to the position of treasurer of the North Coast branch. Not long afterwards he opened a shop, Bambata's Bargain Bazaar, in Stanger, whose name Inkatha had changed to Kwaduguza. You bet there was very little resistance – it wasn't very wise to argue with a 10 000-strong knobkerrie- and spear-wielding impi marching down the main street.

To this day they still talk about the legendary Arunachalam Cup Final in Mount Edgecombe. It was a ding-dong battle and neither side had scored. A goal by Young Springboks was disallowed just before half time, having been adjudged offside. A fight almost broke out but Moosa and Musi were at hand to keep things under control. Then, in the very last minute, Johnny dribbled past Fanyana Ngcobo and was in a perfect position to score. Mount Edgecombe held its collective breath. Just as he readied himself to score what looked like a certain goal, he was brought down from behind in the penalty area. The whole ground shouted 'Penalty!' but the referee ignored the shouts and waved play on. Extra time was taken and there was still no score. Despite some miraculous saves by Black Cat Bambata, the score at the end was 3–3. It was later whispered that someone had bribed the referee. Of course, Chaka Ronnie made a packet. There was a strong suspicion that it was Chaka Ronnie who fixed the game but no one could really prove it. Young Springboks went on to win the replay, with Chaka Ronnie offering odds this time of 5 to 10 on Young Springboks and 2 to 1 on the Rovers. At such attractive odds a lot of money was wagered on the Rovers. Chaka Ronnie once more made a whack when Young Springboks romped home 4-1, thanks to a splendid Johnny Veerappen hat trick.

Years later, good fortune was to smile on Mothie to the extent that he was able to improve his drinking habits considerably. Mothie's three older sons had made enough money from their vegetable hawking stalls at the side of the main road right under the gum tree, despite Mothie's dire warnings that the midnight spook would get them. They made enough money to buy off Bullwa's Farm. They were now supplying vegetables and mandarins to the supermarkets and to the English Market. The remainder was sent to the Indian Market. They bought a ten-roomed house in Avoca with three outhouses, which were all let out. Mothie left his old company house to live with them. Prem won a scholarship and went on to complete his doctorate in Education at the Char Ou's University of Durban-Westville. His dissertation for the degree was: 'The Resonance in Adulthood of the Imagery Employed in Colonial Nursery Rhymes, with Particular Reference to the Rhyme, "Ten Green Bottles".'

Needless to say, there were always ten green bottles of Scotch in his liquor cabinet, which (again needless to say) with Premwa's blessings was regularly visited by his adoring pater Mothie, now having abandoned his taste for cheap wine. Mothie's bites remained the same, chilli bites instead of the olives, or cheese and biscuits, favoured by his son. However he never stopped complaining about 'nowaday's chilli-bites'. He would mutter fondly, 'Can't beat Chinamma's chilli-bites, I tell you!'

As for Sunny, fortune was to smile on him in the most unexpected way. In the Seventies, international sanctions began to hit the lahnee Wit Ous where it hurt most – in the pocket. They realised that they stood to lose a lot of money if they continued to cling to their pigmentocracy. They just had to cross the Rubicon to avoid being stranded on the wrong shore. It dawned on them that despite Ronnie Reagan's and Maggie Thatcher's policies of Constructive Engagement they couldn't fool the world any longer. Just when everyone expected their leader, the Groot Krokodil, to wade across that boundary, the finger-wagging head honcho of the rocks and the rooineks instead lamely opted to make window-dressing concessions. He was backed by one Amichand Rajbansi, thick-skinned head of the roundly rejected, subservient Char Ous' Parliament, the House of Delegates, which, rather unkindly, became known as the House of Dele-Goats; and also backed by the swimming supremo of yesteryear, the Reverend Allan Hendrickse of the Bruin Ous' Parliament, the equally rejected House of Representatives. Rajbansi was later to double-cross the 1994 bridge and got into bed with the ANC. He was promptly rewarded by being made Minister of Sports in KwaZulu-Natal, although the phrase 'fair play' was missing from his dictionary. He was roundly applauded by his one-time adversary, Pat Poovalingum in his weekly tabloid column. However, one of the concessions made by the Groot Krokodil before all this could happen was that Char Ous and Bruin Ous were now given the right to own liquor licences. At the same time Mount Edgecombe was declared a Char Ous' area and the White House Hotel was put up for sale.

Mr So-So was dumped and, after drinking away his lump-sum severance pay and most of his early pension package, ended up becoming an inmate of the Salvation Army Relief Hostel. To while away the time he learnt to play the accordion, giving a stirring rendition of 'God Save the Queen' when the occasion arose, and sometimes when it didn't. The hostel, like other such institutions in the New South Africa, was now nonracial. He still pointed his consonants and rounded his vowels on the odd occasion. For fellow Indian inmates who shared their dop with him he would play a reasonable version of the hit-song 'Khabi Khabi', especially after a hot cup of russum, which he learnt to make himself.

There was fierce bidding for the White House Hotel. The Naidoo brothers, represented by Bertie and his younger brother, well known as LM, one of many families who had pulled themselves up by their own bootstraps, eventually won the bid. They appointed Sunny Chellakooty as manager. Although the Stranger did put his foot back at the White House Hotel for a few drinks after Johnny's wedding, it was for the last time. It must not be forgotten it was the White House Hotel of the Old South Africa we were talking about previously. But now this was the White House Hotel of the New South Africa. And what's more, he was treated to drinks in the lounge by the new manager, Sunny Chellakooty, whose consonants and vowels, despite a distinct nasal tincture, were just as pointed and rounded as his former lahnee's was as he yelled at some unfortunate vassal, 'You Blithering Idiot!' Sunny was also now able to step up his fiddling considerably. He could introduce not one but two of his own bottles into the stock almost at will, although he took care, as he had done throughout his career, not to overdo it. He was firmly of the view that if you overdid anything, your karma would catch up with you. Indeed he had honed his skills so finely that he never got caught. Crime, in this instance, paid handsomely. Soon he was able to move out of the family's company house into a brand new house in Phoenix. He was also able to trade in his beloved Morris Thousand for a late model Datsun Thirteen Hundred.

There was another important change in the new South Africa. Char Ous could now have book-makers licences. Chaka Ronnie took full advantage – he took out a licence with the name, Honest Chaka Ronnie. By now the racing industry had wised up to the Bag Boys. They posed a major threat to the shareholders and had to be eliminated. At the very last minute before the start of a race, word went out to the jockey of the horse that the Bag Boys had placed their money on. At the same time, the syndicates withdrew their bets by courtesy of the bookies although this was illegal. They also withdrew their bets on the Tote. The favourite didn't even finish in the first three with the result that the Bag Boys continued to lose heavily. Chaka Ronnie saw it coming and he was quick to change sides which was why he had greater motivation to take out his own licence.

Impressed by the Naidoos' doggedness, in the face of stiff competition, to buy the White House Hotel, the former owners, the Hulett Sugar Company, were curious to know why the family were so hell bent on buying it. The incoming company's newly appointed CEO, Luxmiah Markandayar Naidoo, pointing to the cane fields through the window of the upstairs lounge of the White House Hotel, said, 'Our forebears used to slave on those fields. We are revisiting the scene of the crime.'

Other titles available from Jacana

Song of the Atman
by Ronnie Govender

Saving the Zululand Wilderness:
An Early Struggle for Nature Conservation
by Donal P. McCracken

Hunger for Freedom:
The Story of Food in the Life of Nelson Mandela
by Anna Trapido

Love and Courage:
A Story of Insubordination
by Pregs Govender

The ANC Underground in South Africa
by Raymond Suttner

Great Lives:
Pivotal Moments
by Lauren Segal and Paul Holden